NO
A
RANG

D0571114

BATMAN TEENAGE MUTANT NINJA TURTLES ADVENTURES

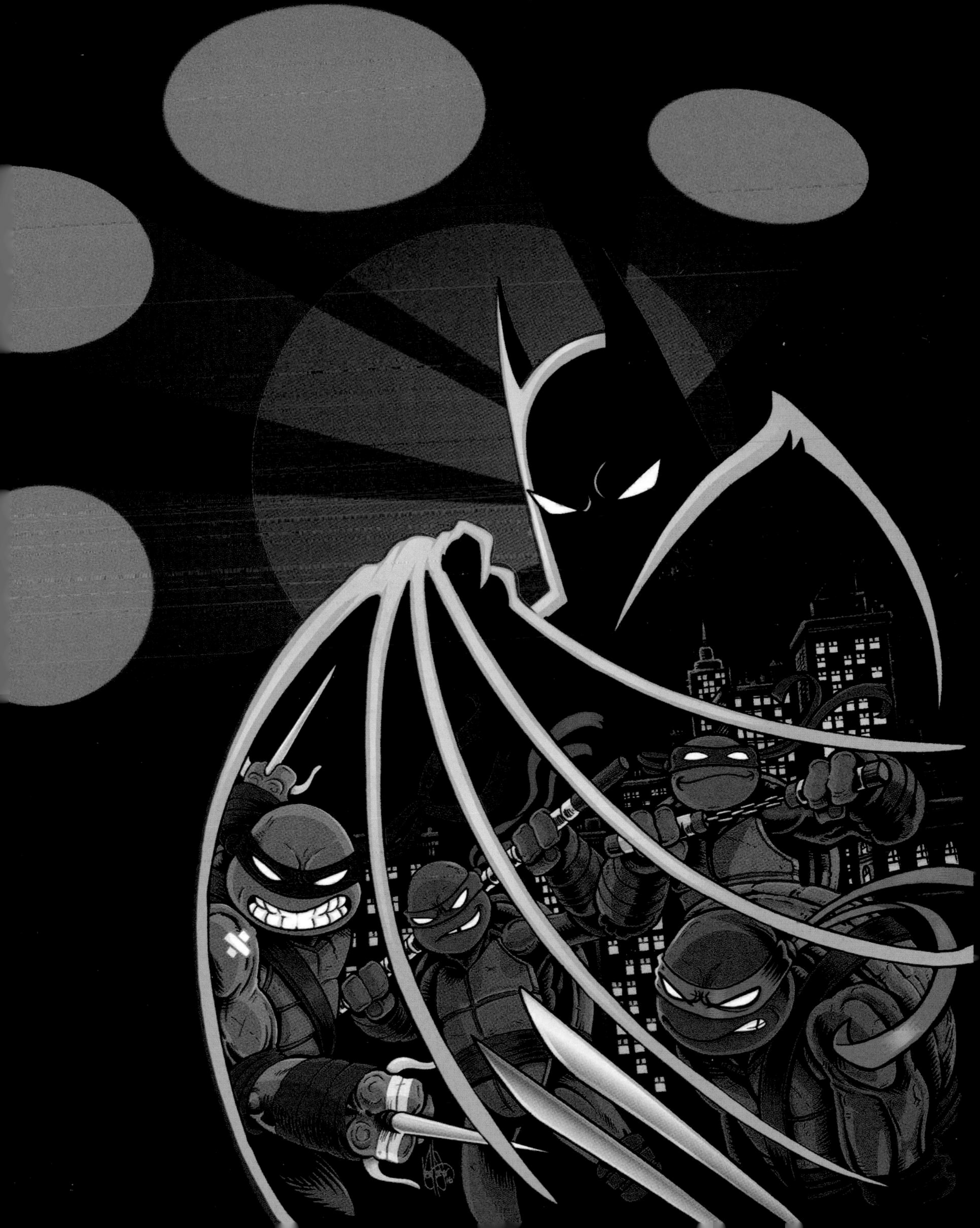

Batman / Teenage Mutant Ninja Turtles Adventures
is published by Stone Arch Books,
A Capstone Imprint
1710 Roe Crest Drive
North Mankato, Minnesota 56003
www.mycapstonepub.com

BATMAN/TEENAGE MUTANT NINJA TURTLES ADVENTURES.
JULY 2017. FIRST PRINTING. © 2019 Viacom
International Inc. and DC Comics. All Rights Reserved.
Nickelodeon, TEENAGE MUTANT NINJA TURTLES, and all
related titles, logos and characters are trademarks
of Viacom International Inc. © 2019 Viacom Overseas
Holdings C.V. All Rights Reserved. Nickelodeon,
TEENAGE MUTANT NINJA TURTLES, and all related titles,
logos and characters are trademarks of Viacom
Overseas Holdings C.V. Based on characters created
by Peter Laird and Kevin Eastman. DC LOGO, BATMAN
and all related characters and elements © & ™
DC Comics. All Rights Reserved. © 2019 Idea and
Design Works, LLC. The IDW logo is registered in the
U.S. Patent and Trademark Office. IDW Publishing,
a division of Idea and Design Works, LLC. Editorial
offices: 2765 Truxtun Road, San Diego, CA 92106. Any
similarities to persons living or dead are purely
coincidental. With the exception of artwork used
for review purposes, none of the contents of this
publication may be reprinted without the permission
of Idea and Design Works, LLC. Printed in Korea.
IDW Publishing does not read or accept unsolicited
submissions of ideas, stories, or artwork.

Originally published as BATMAN/TEENAGE MUTANT NINJA
TURTLES ADVENTURES issue #6.

Special thanks to Jim Chadwick, Joan Hilty, Linda Lee,
and Kat van Dam for their invaluable assistance.
All rights reserved. No part of this publication may
be produced in whole or in part, or stored in a
retrieval system, or transmitted in any form or by
any means, electronic, mechanical, photocopying,
recording, or otherwise, without written permissions
of the publisher.

Cataloging-in-Publication Data is available at the
Library of Congress website:
ISBN 978-1-4965-7387-2 (library binding)
ISBN 978-1-4965-7394-0 (eBook PDF)

Summary: When the Kraang attack Gotham City,
Batman and the Teenage Mutant Ninja Turtles team
up with an old enemy.

STONE ARCH BOOKS
Donald Lemke Editorial Director
Gena Chester Editor
Hilary Wacholz Art Director
Kathy McColley Production Specialist

Batman created by Bob Kane with Bill Finger

BATMAN TEENAGE MUTANT NINJA TURTLES ADVENTURES

THE TERROR OF THE KRAANG

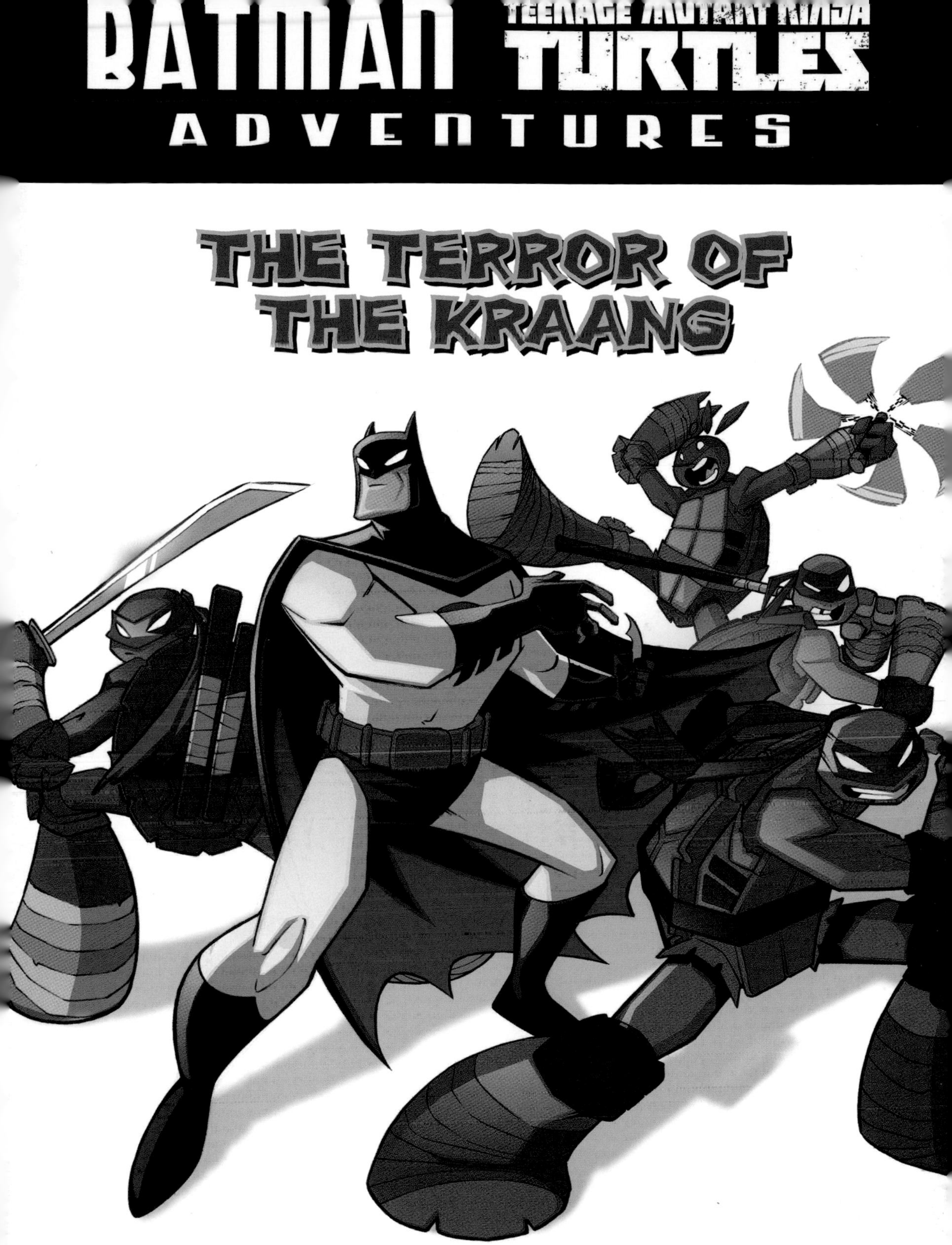

WRITER: MATTHEW K. MANNING | ARTIST: JON SOMMARIVA
INKER: SEAN PARSONS | COLORIST: LEONARDO ITO

STONE ARCH BOOKS
a capstone imprint

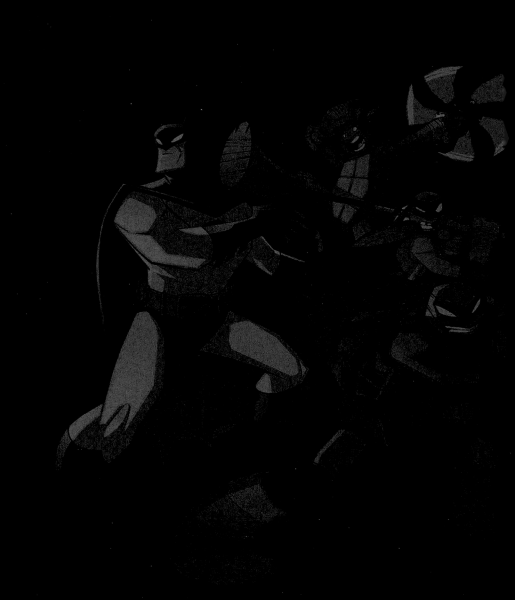

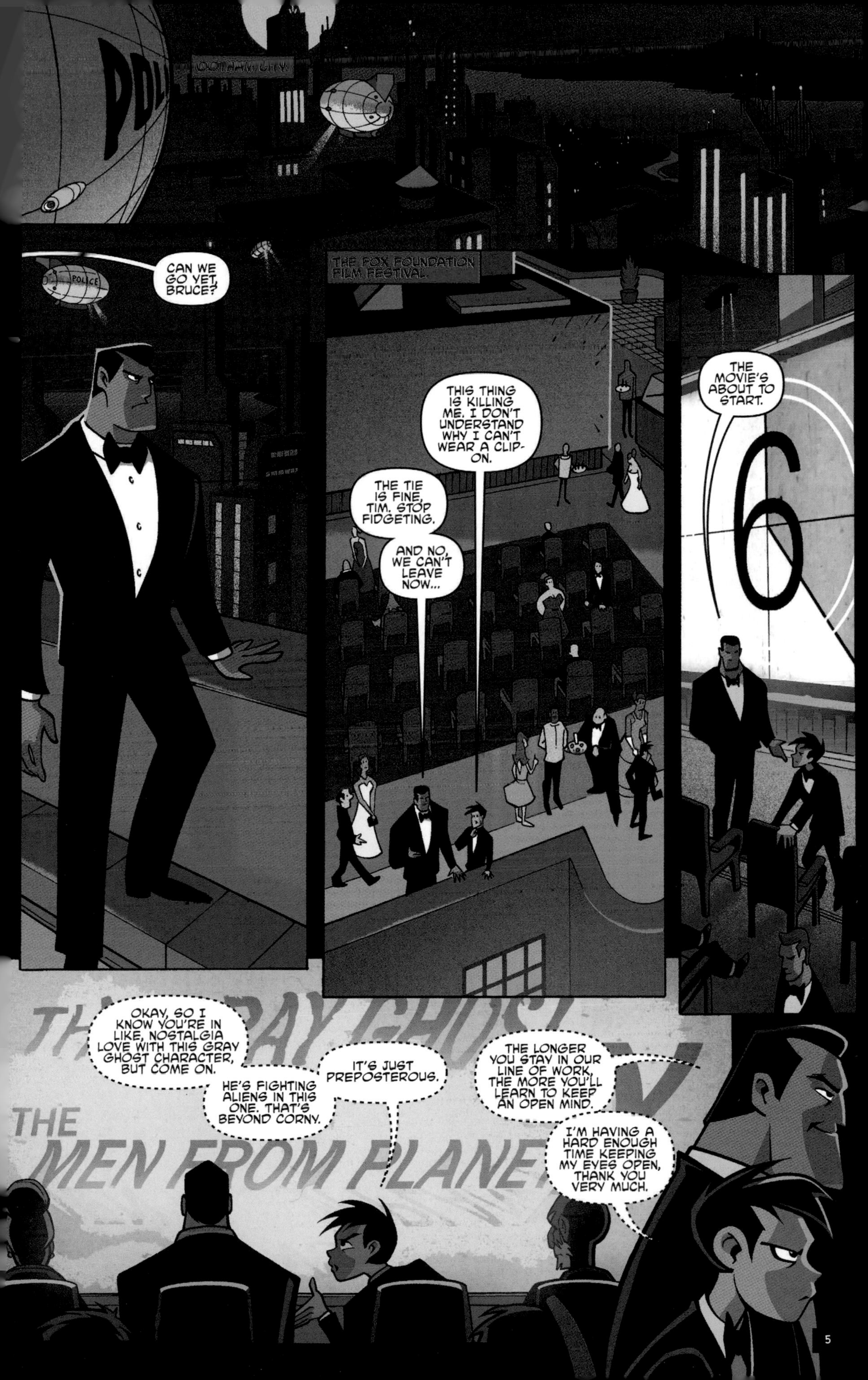
GOTHAM CITY
POLICE
CAN WE GO YET, BRUCE?
THE FOX FOUNDATION FILM FESTIVAL
THIS THING IS KILLING ME. I DON'T UNDERSTAND WHY I CAN'T WEAR A CLIP-ON.
THE TIE IS FINE, TIM. STOP FIDGETING.
AND NO, WE CAN'T LEAVE NOW...
THE MOVIE'S ABOUT TO START.
6
THE
MEN FROM PLANE
OKAY, SO I KNOW YOU'RE IN LIKE, NOSTALGIA LOVE WITH THIS GRAY GHOST CHARACTER, BUT COME ON.
HE'S FIGHTING ALIENS IN THIS ONE. THAT'S BEYOND CORNY.
IT'S JUST PREPOSTEROUS.
THE LONGER YOU STAY IN OUR LINE OF WORK, THE MORE YOU'LL LEARN TO KEEP AN OPEN MIND.
I'M HAVING A HARD ENOUGH TIME KEEPING MY EYES OPEN, THANK YOU VERY MUCH.

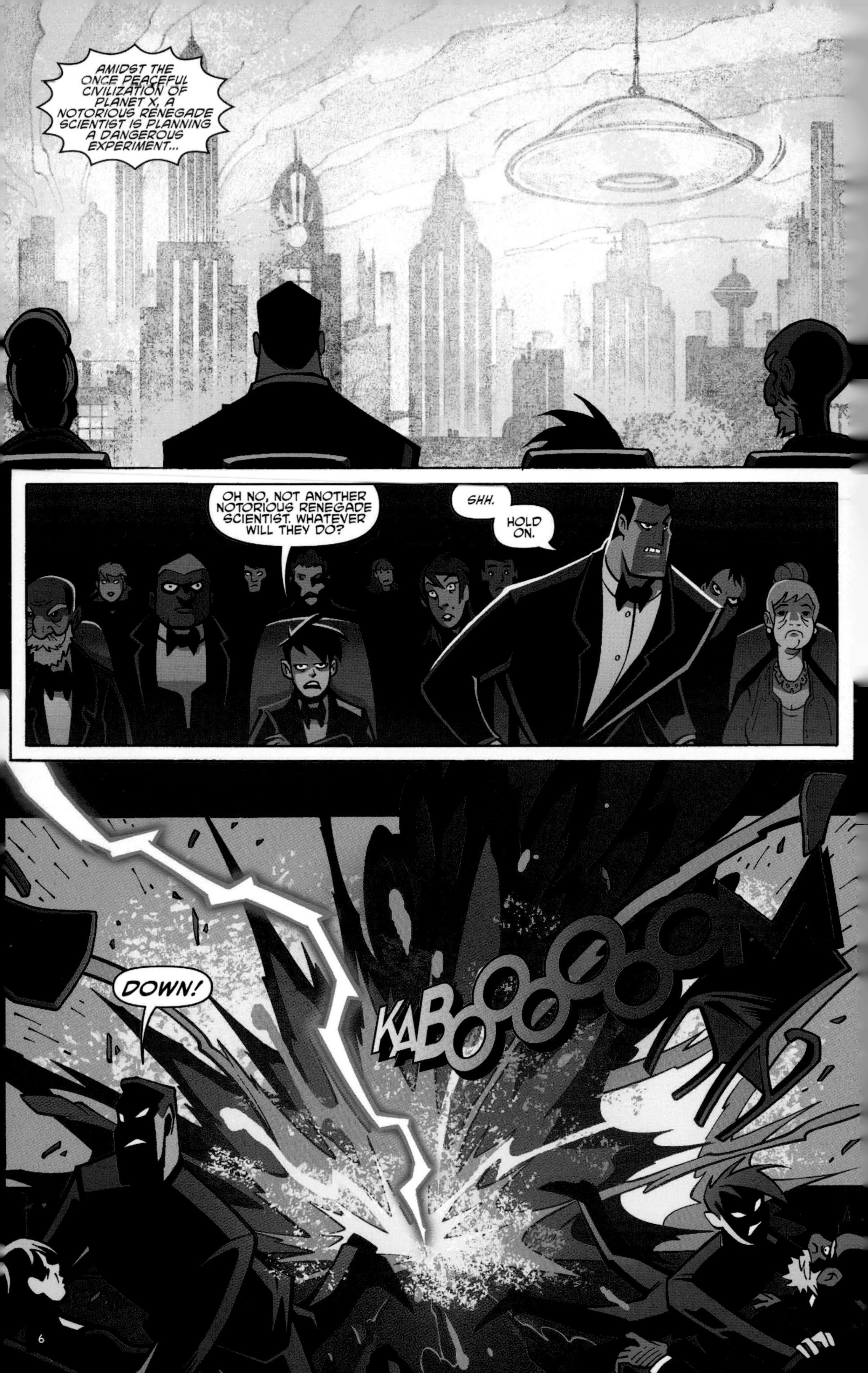
AMIDST THE ONCE PEACEFUL CIVILIZATION OF PLANET X, A NOTORIOUS RENEGADE SCIENTIST IS PLANNING A DANGEROUS EXPERIMENT...
OH NO, NOT ANOTHER NOTORIOUS RENEGADE SCIENTIST. WHATEVER WILL THEY DO?
SHH.
HOLD ON.
DOWN!
KABOOOOOOOM

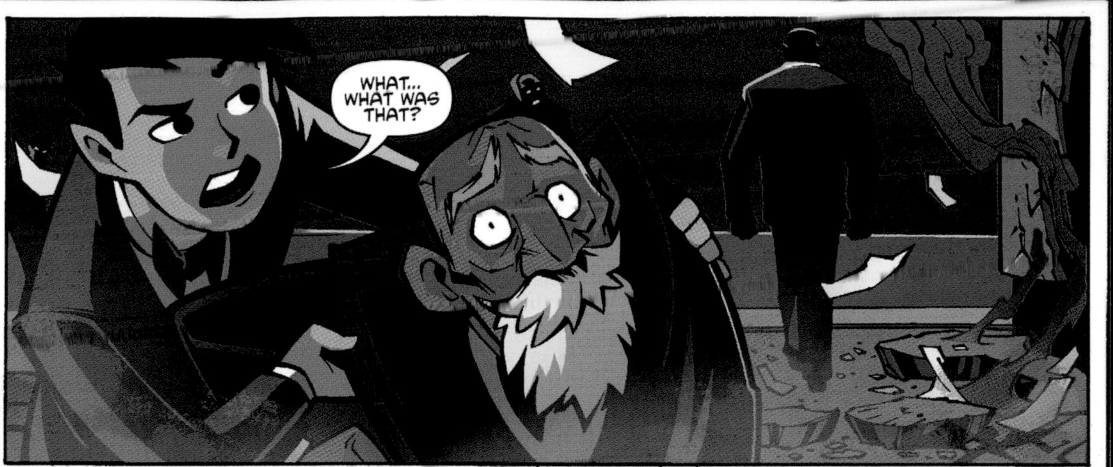
WHAT... WHAT WAS THAT?

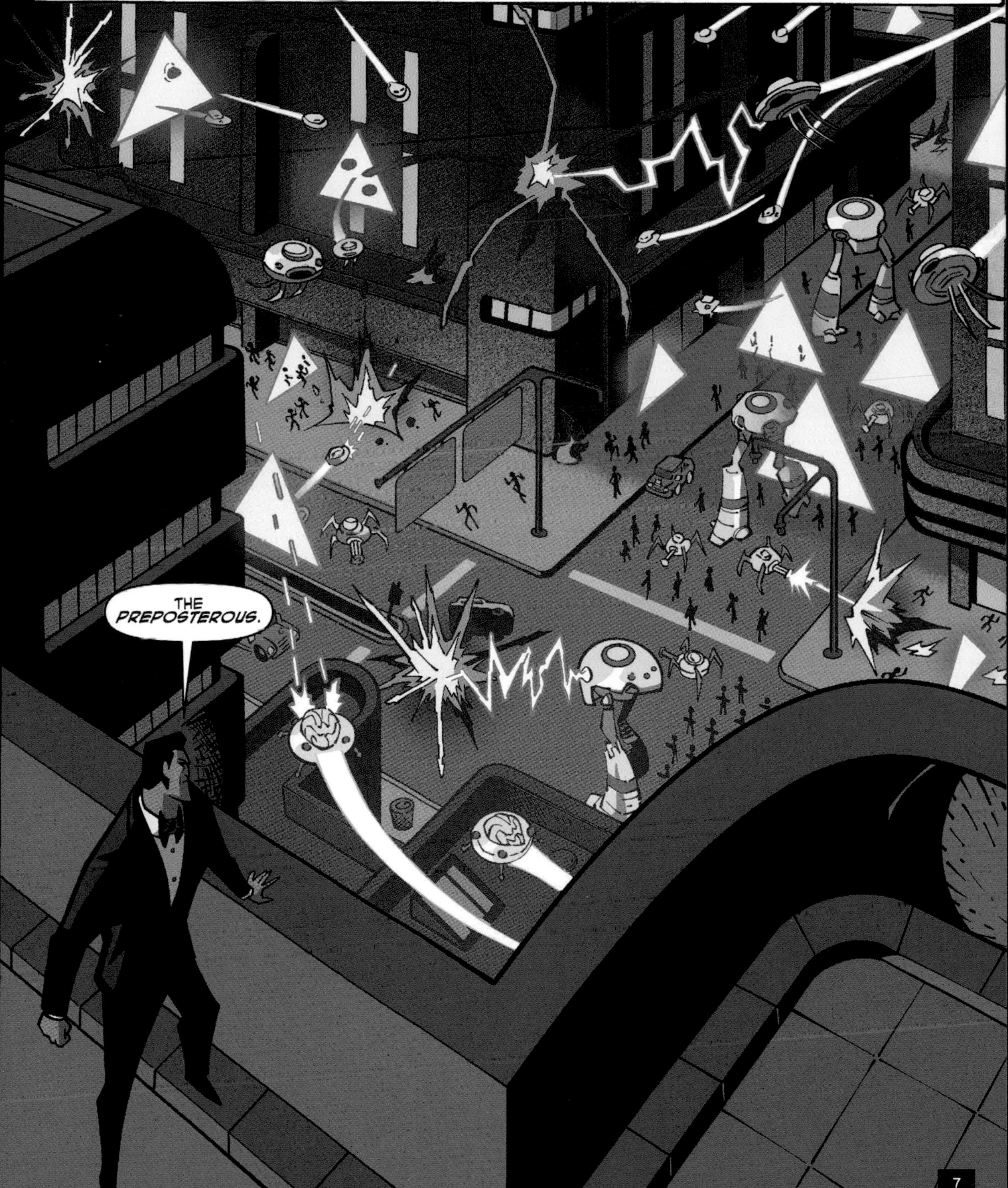
THE *PREPOSTEROUS.*

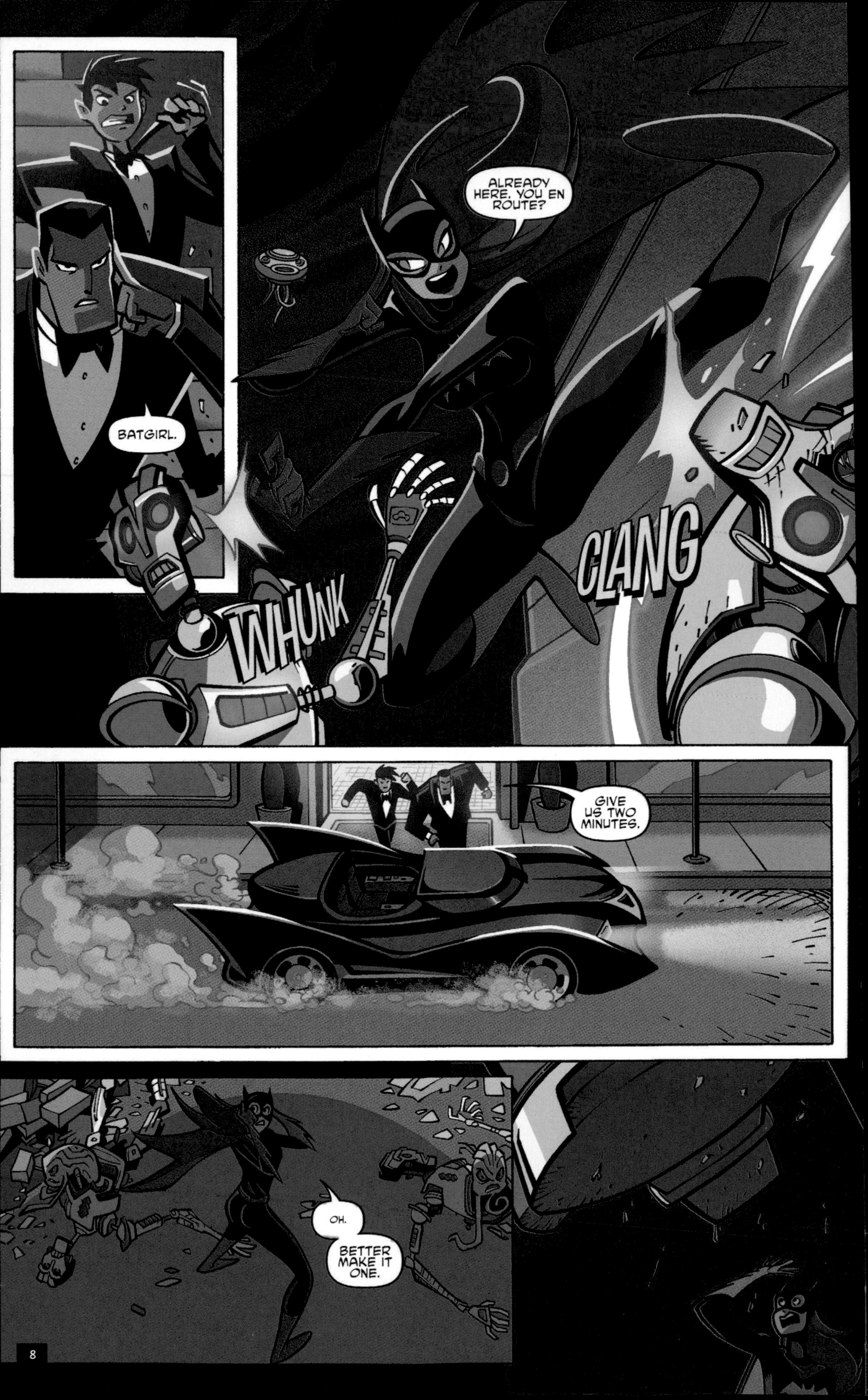
ALREADY HERE. YOU EN ROUTE?
BATGIRL.
WHUNK
CLANG
GIVE US TWO MINUTES.
OH.
BETTER MAKE IT ONE.

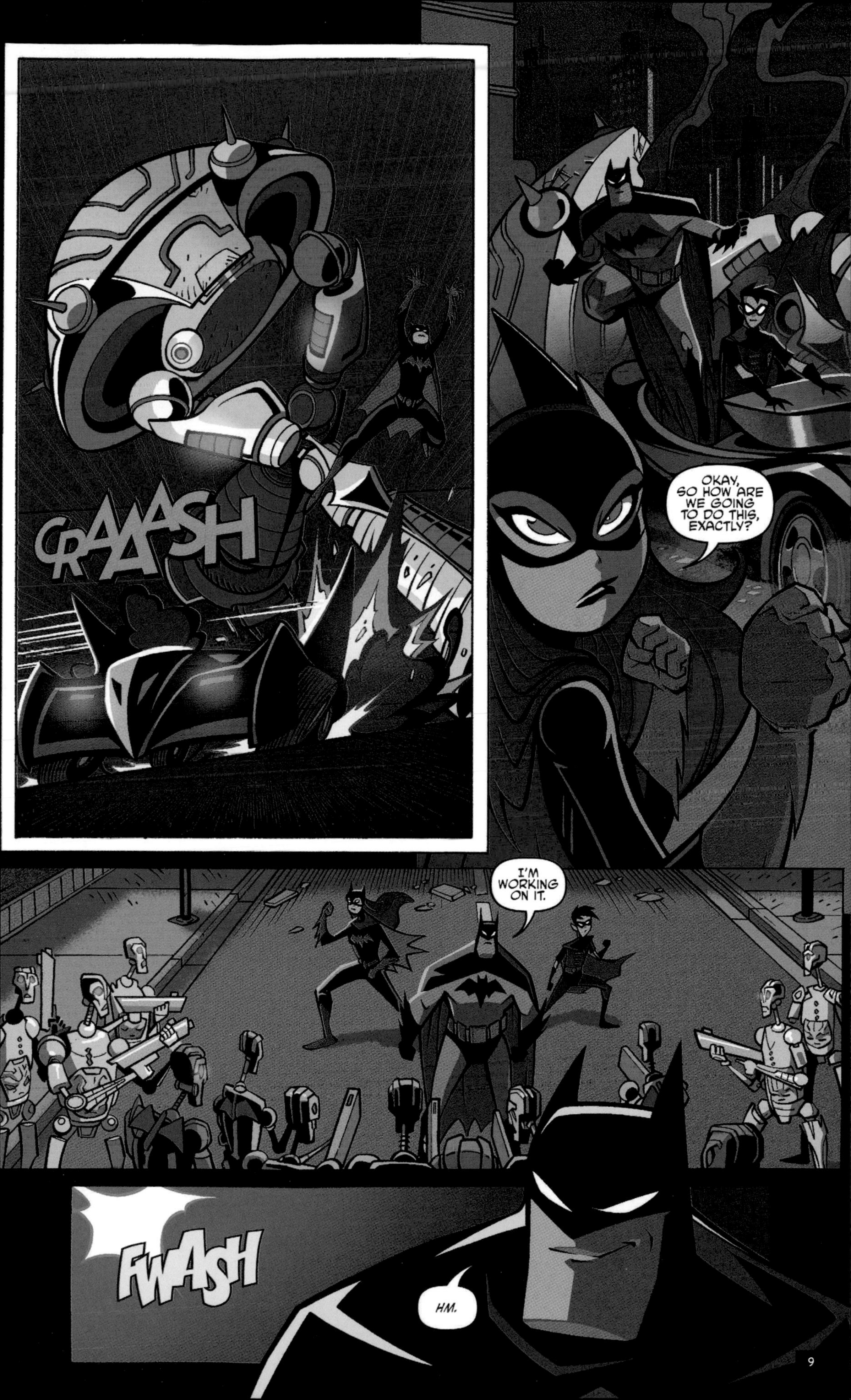
CRAAASH
OKAY, SO HOW ARE WE GOING TO DO THIS, EXACTLY?
I'M WORKING ON IT.
FWASH
HM.

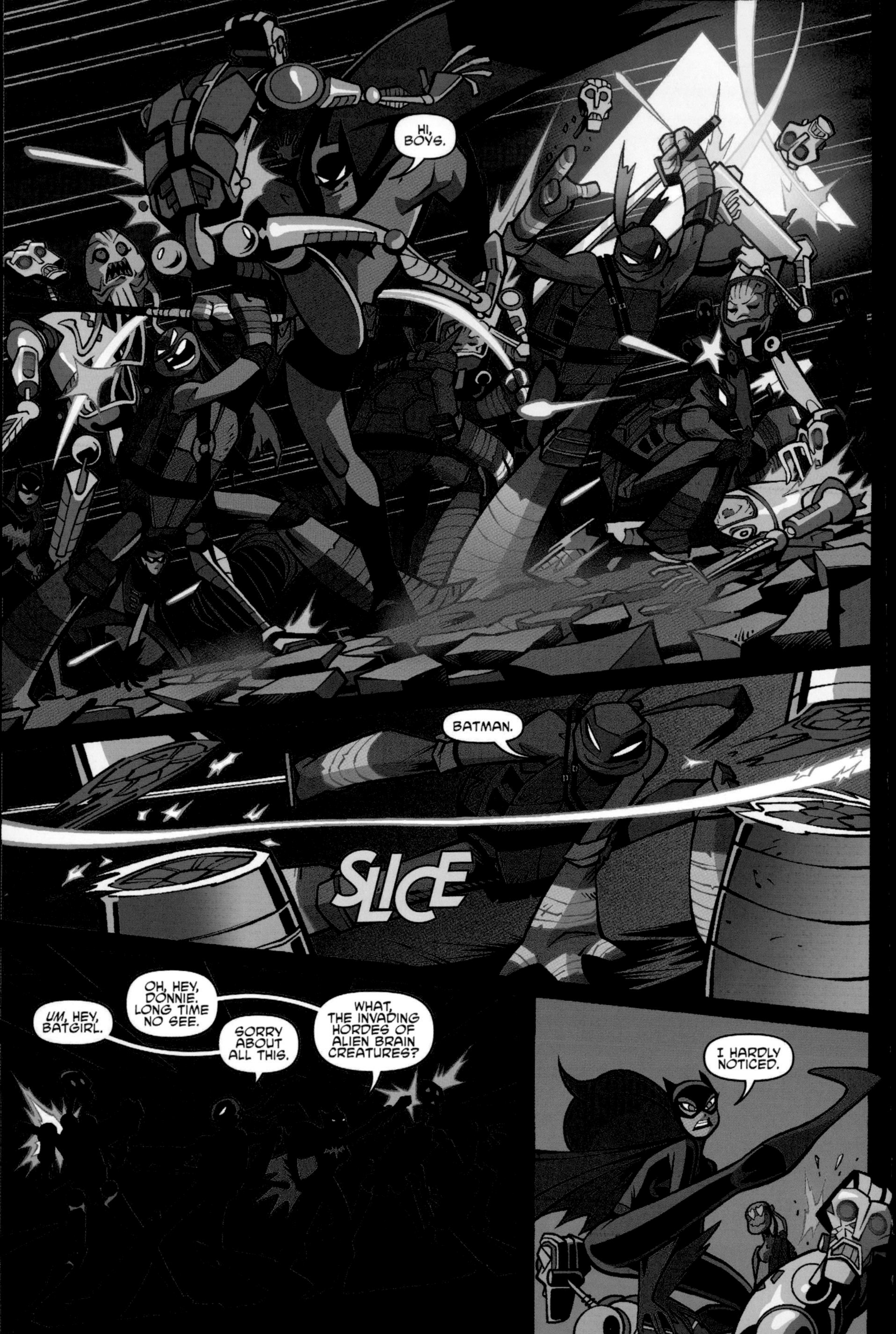
HI, BOYS.
BATMAN.
SLICE
UM, HEY, BATGIRL.
OH, HEY, DONNIE. LONG TIME NO SEE.
SORRY ABOUT ALL THIS.
WHAT, THE INVADING HORDES OF ALIEN BRAIN CREATURES?
I HARDLY NOTICED.

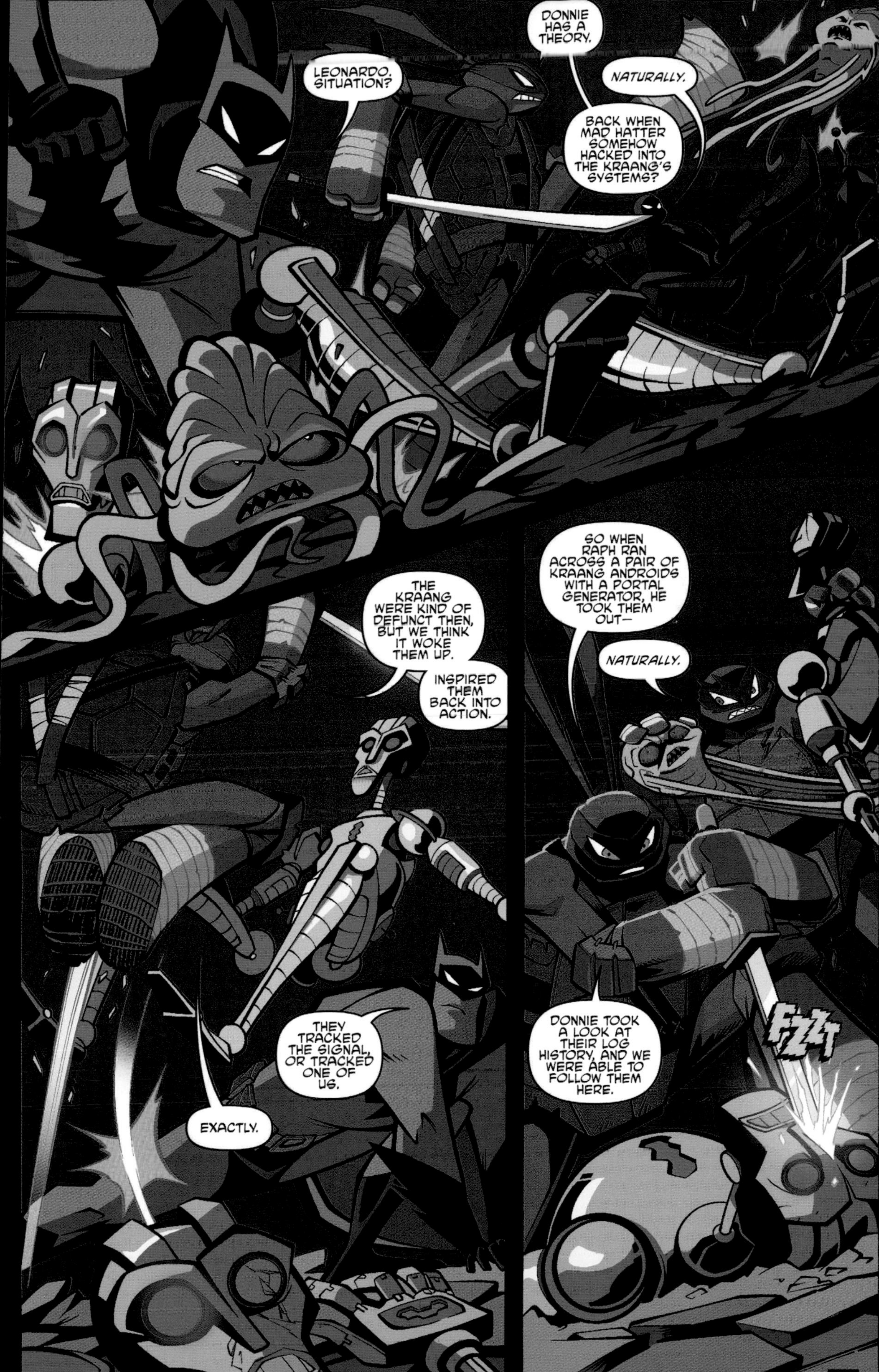
LEONARDO. SITUATION?
DONNIE HAS A THEORY.
NATURALLY.
BACK WHEN MAD HATTER SOMEHOW HACKED INTO THE KRAANG'S SYSTEMS?
THE KRAANG WERE KIND OF DEFUNCT THEN, BUT WE THINK IT WOKE THEM UP.
INSPIRED THEM BACK INTO ACTION.
THEY TRACKED THE SIGNAL, OR TRACKED ONE OF US.
EXACTLY.
SO WHEN RAPH RAN ACROSS A PAIR OF KRAANG ANDROIDS WITH A PORTAL GENERATOR, HE TOOK THEM OUT—
NATURALLY.
DONNIE TOOK A LOOK AT THEIR LOG HISTORY, AND WE WERE ABLE TO FOLLOW THEM HERE.
FZZZT

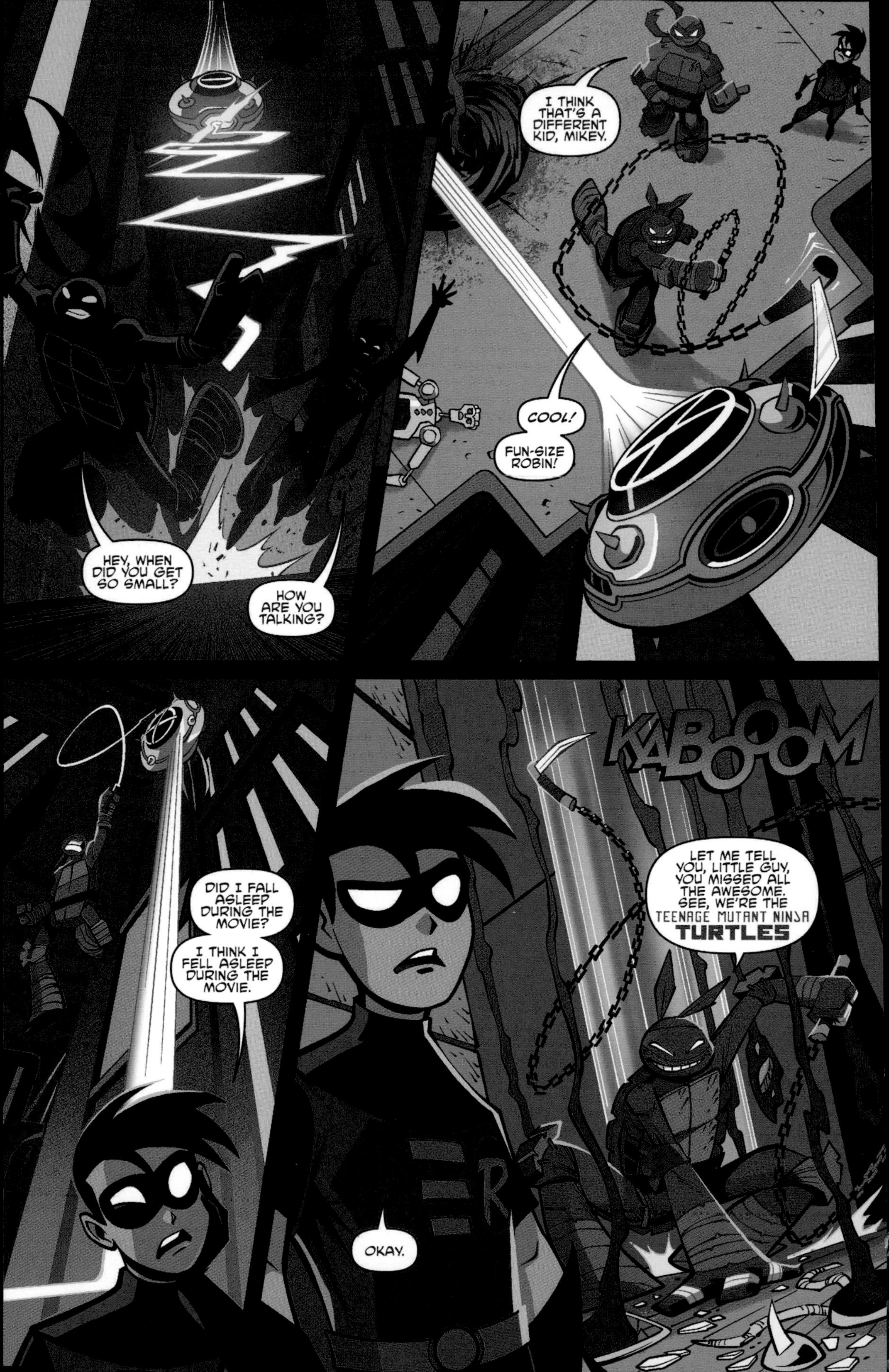
HEY, WHEN DID YOU GET SO SMALL?
HOW ARE YOU TALKING?
COOL!
FUN-SIZE ROBIN!
I THINK THAT'S A DIFFERENT KID, MIKEY.
DID I FALL ASLEEP DURING THE MOVIE?
I THINK I FELL ASLEEP DURING THE MOVIE.
OKAY.
KABOOOM
LET ME TELL YOU, LITTLE GUY, YOU MISSED ALL THE AWESOME. SEE, WE'RE THE TEENAGE MUTANT NINJA TURTLES

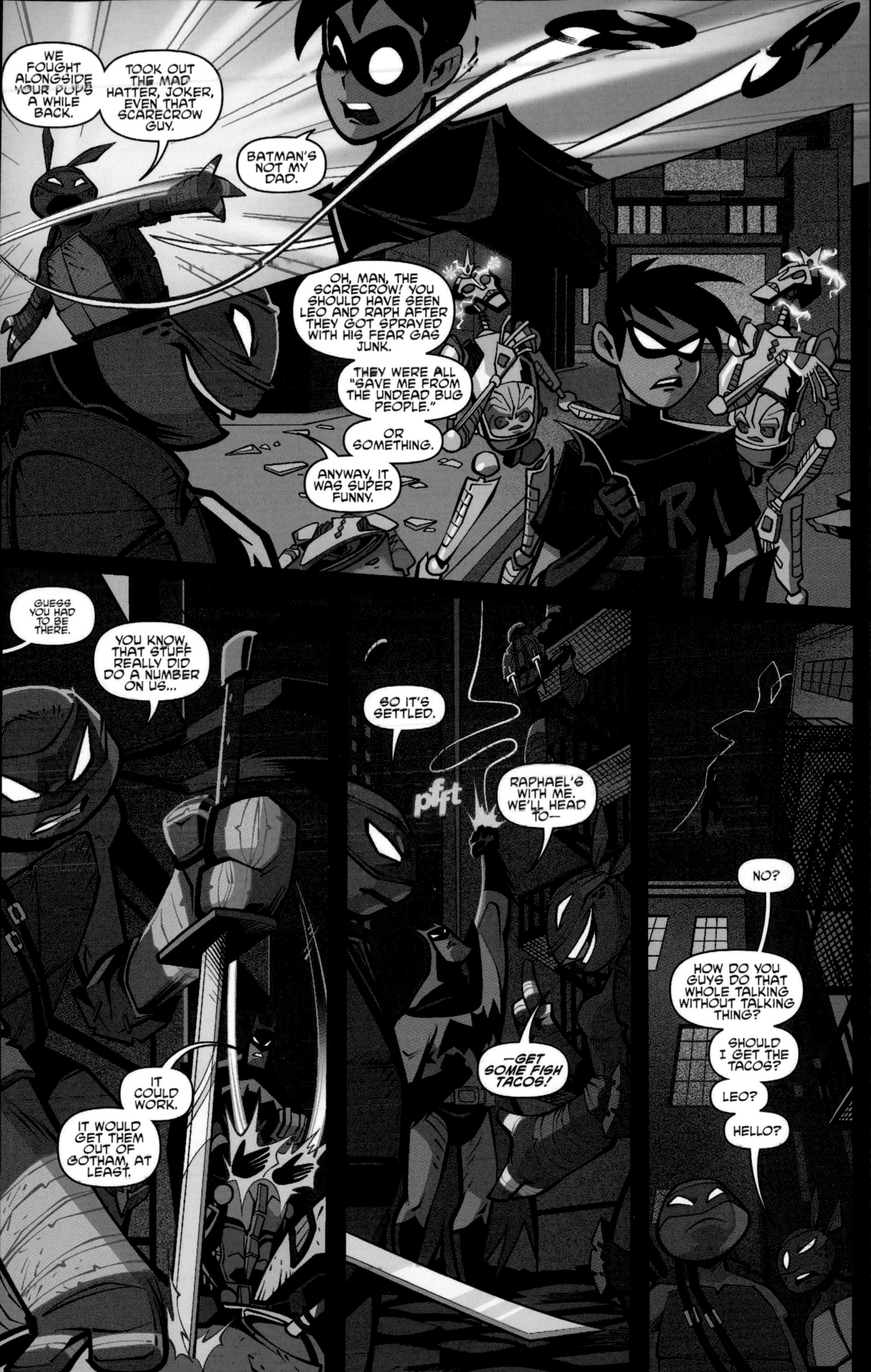
WE FOUGHT ALONGSIDE YOUR PUPS A WHILE BACK.
TOOK OUT THE MAD HATTER, JOKER, EVEN THAT SCARECROW GUY.
BATMAN'S NOT MY DAD.
OH, MAN, THE SCARECROW! YOU SHOULD HAVE SEEN LEO AND RAPH AFTER THEY GOT SPRAYED WITH HIS FEAR GAS JUNK.
THEY WERE ALL "SAVE ME FROM THE UNDEAD BUG PEOPLE."
OR SOMETHING.
ANYWAY, IT WAS SUPER FUNNY.
GUESS YOU HAD TO BE THERE.
YOU KNOW, THAT STUFF REALLY DID DO A NUMBER ON US...
IT COULD WORK.
IT WOULD GET THEM OUT OF GOTHAM, AT LEAST.
SO IT'S SETTLED.
pfft
RAPHAEL'S WITH ME. WE'LL HEAD TO—
—GET SOME FISH TACOS!
NO?
HOW DO YOU GUYS DO THAT WHOLE TALKING WITHOUT TALKING THING?
SHOULD I GET THE TACOS?
LEO?
HELLO?

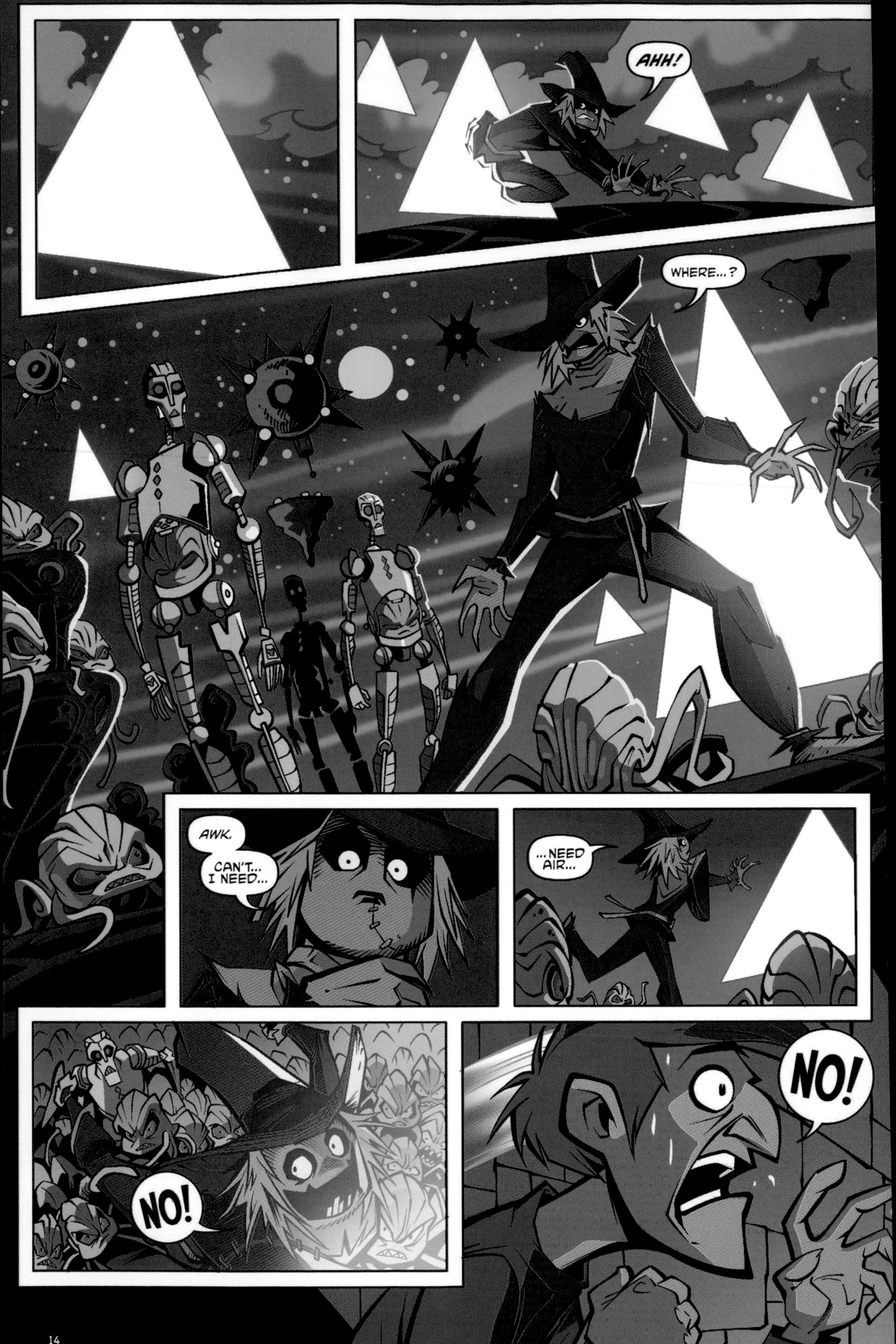
AHH!
WHERE...?
AWK.
CAN'T... I NEED...
...NEED AIR...
NO!
NO!

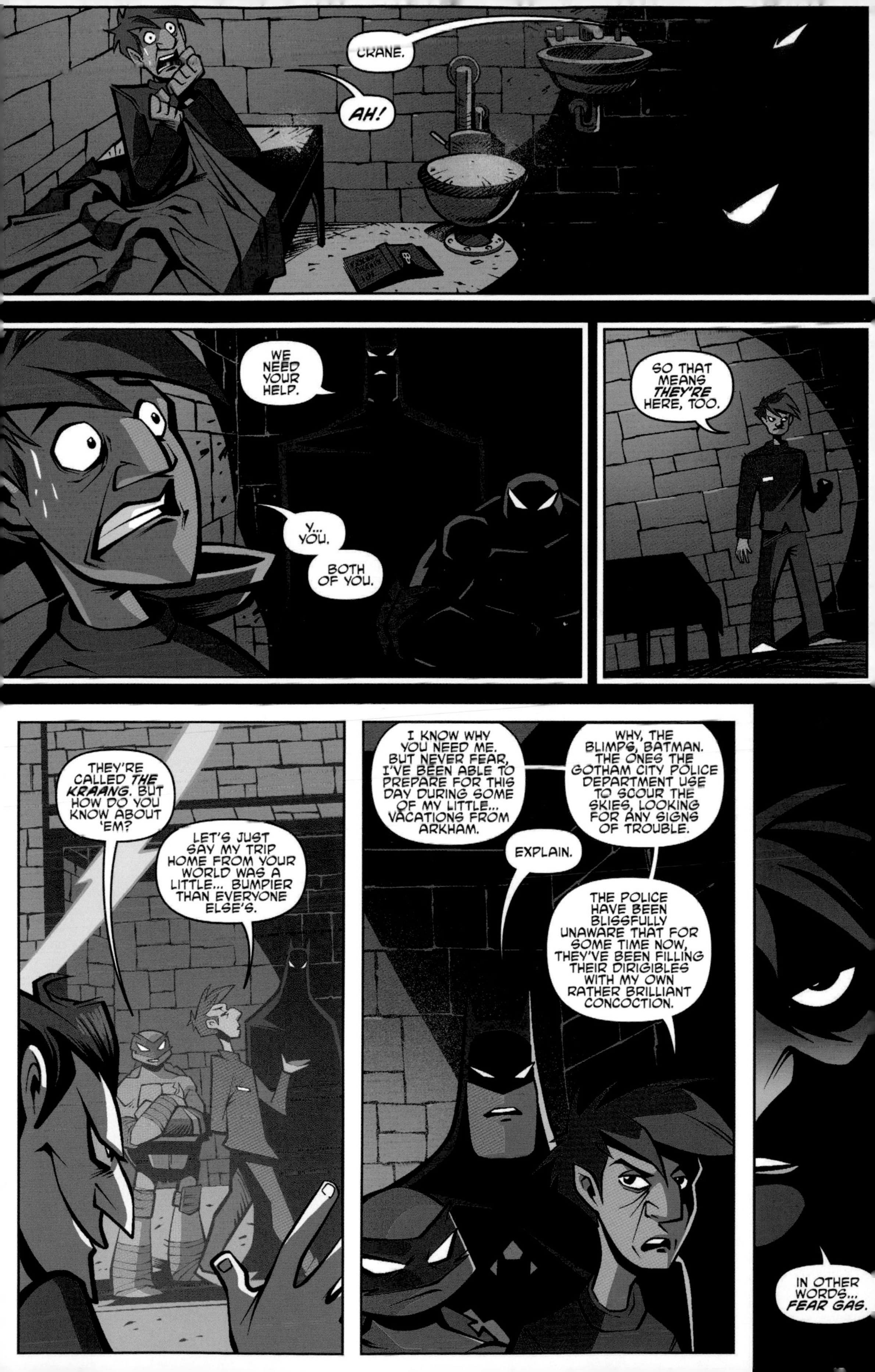
CRANE.
AH!
WE NEED YOUR HELP.
Y... YOU.
BOTH OF YOU.
SO THAT MEANS THEY'RE HERE, TOO.
THEY'RE CALLED THE KRAANG. BUT HOW DO YOU KNOW ABOUT 'EM?
LET'S JUST SAY MY TRIP HOME FROM YOUR WORLD WAS A LITTLE... BUMPIER THAN EVERYONE ELSE'S.
I KNOW WHY YOU NEED ME. BUT NEVER FEAR, I'VE BEEN ABLE TO PREPARE FOR THIS DAY DURING SOME OF MY LITTLE... VACATIONS FROM ARKHAM.
WHY, THE BLIMPS, BATMAN. THE ONES THE GOTHAM CITY POLICE DEPARTMENT USE TO SCOUR THE SKIES, LOOKING FOR ANY SIGNS OF TROUBLE.
EXPLAIN.
THE POLICE HAVE BEEN BLISSFULLY UNAWARE THAT FOR SOME TIME NOW, THEY'VE BEEN FILLING THEIR DIRIGIBLES WITH MY OWN RATHER BRILLIANT CONCOCTION.
IN OTHER WORDS... FEAR GAS.

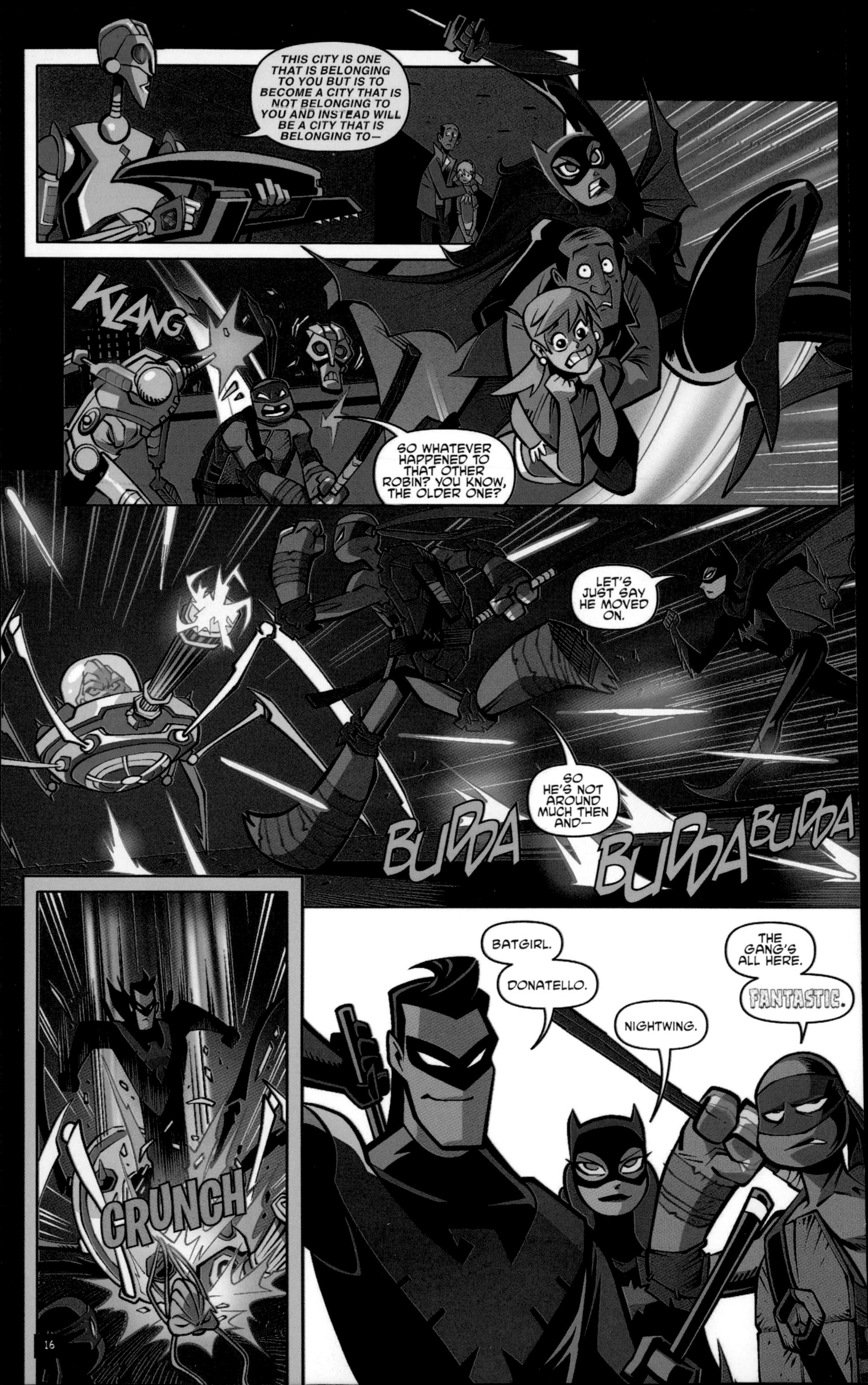
THIS CITY IS ONE THAT IS BELONGING TO YOU BUT IS TO BECOME A CITY THAT IS NOT BELONGING TO YOU AND INSTEAD WILL BE A CITY THAT IS BELONGING TO—
KLANG
SO WHATEVER HAPPENED TO THAT OTHER ROBIN? YOU KNOW, THE OLDER ONE?
LET'S JUST SAY HE MOVED ON.
SO HE'S NOT AROUND MUCH THEN AND—
BUDDA
BUDDA BUDDA
CRUNCH
BATGIRL.
DONATELLO.
NIGHTWING.
THE GANG'S ALL HERE.
FANTASTIC.
16

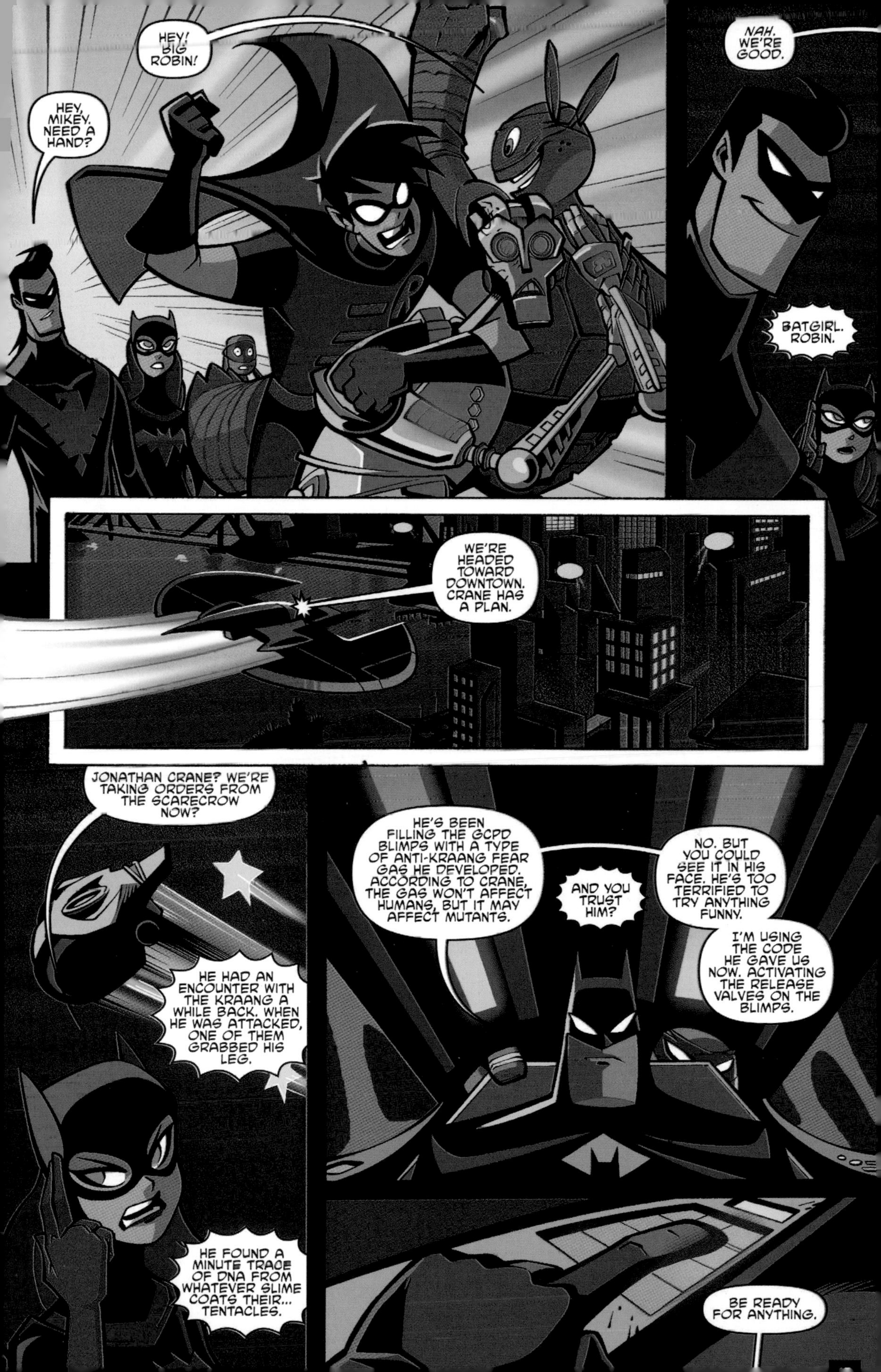
HEY! BIG ROBIN!
HEY, MIKEY. NEED A HAND?
NAH. WE'RE GOOD.
BATGIRL. ROBIN.
WE'RE HEADED TOWARD DOWNTOWN. CRANE HAS A PLAN.
JONATHAN CRANE? WE'RE TAKING ORDERS FROM THE SCARECROW NOW?
HE HAD AN ENCOUNTER WITH THE KRAANG A WHILE BACK. WHEN HE WAS ATTACKED, ONE OF THEM GRABBED HIS LEG.
HE FOUND A MINUTE TRACE OF DNA FROM WHATEVER SLIME COATS THEIR... TENTACLES.
HE'S BEEN FILLING THE GCPD BLIMPS WITH A TYPE OF ANTI-KRAANG FEAR GAS HE DEVELOPED. ACCORDING TO CRANE, THE GAS WON'T AFFECT HUMANS, BUT IT MAY AFFECT MUTANTS.
AND YOU TRUST HIM?
NO. BUT YOU COULD SEE IT IN HIS FACE. HE'S TOO TERRIFIED TO TRY ANYTHING FUNNY.
I'M USING THE CODE HE GAVE US NOW. ACTIVATING THE RELEASE VALVES ON THE BLIMPS.
BE READY FOR ANYTHING.

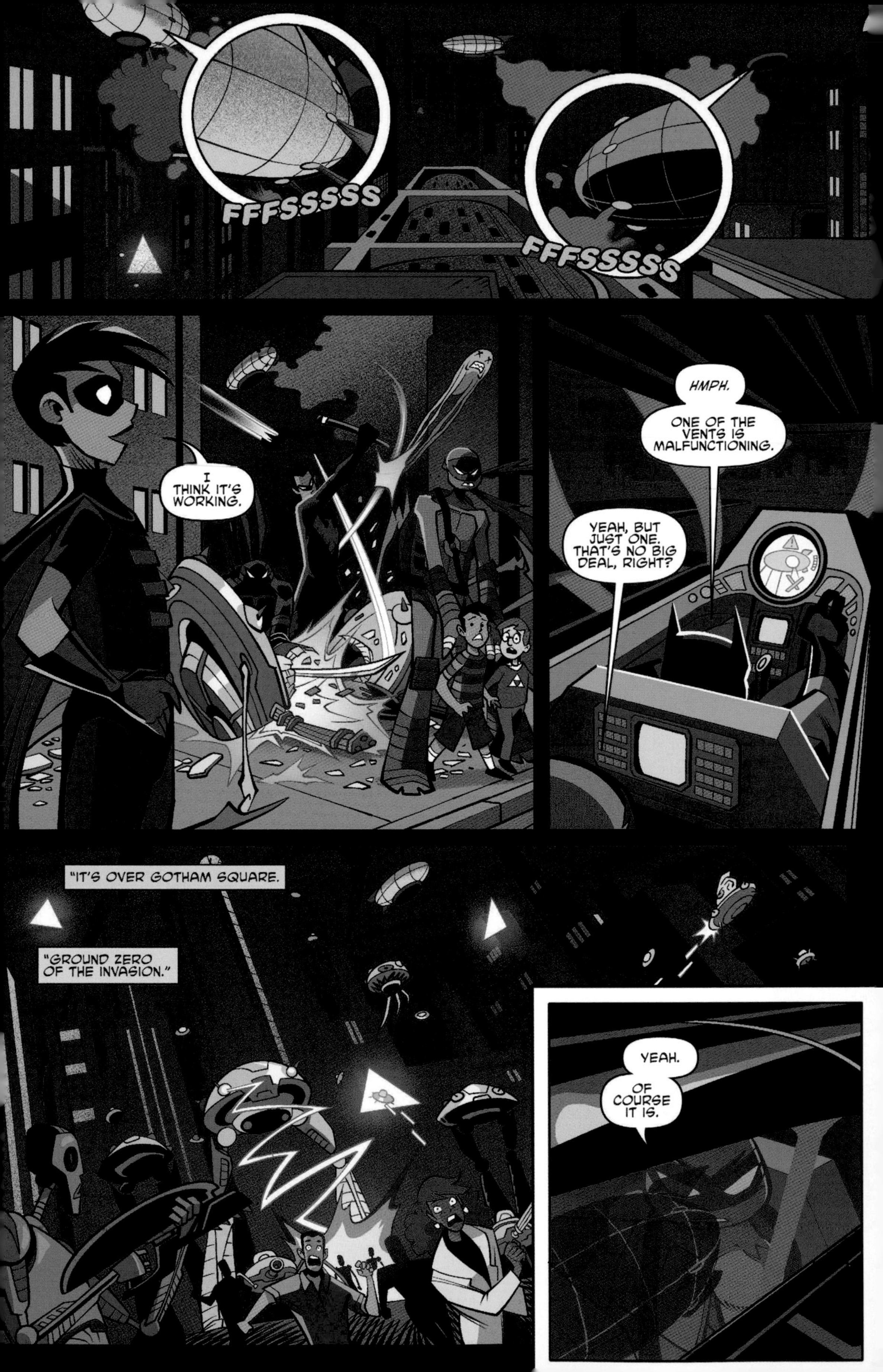
FFFSSSSS
FFFSSSSS
I THINK IT'S WORKING.
HMPH.
ONE OF THE VENTS IS MALFUNCTIONING.
YEAH, BUT JUST ONE. THAT'S NO BIG DEAL, RIGHT?
"IT'S OVER GOTHAM SQUARE.
"GROUND ZERO OF THE INVASION."
YEAH.
OF COURSE IT IS.

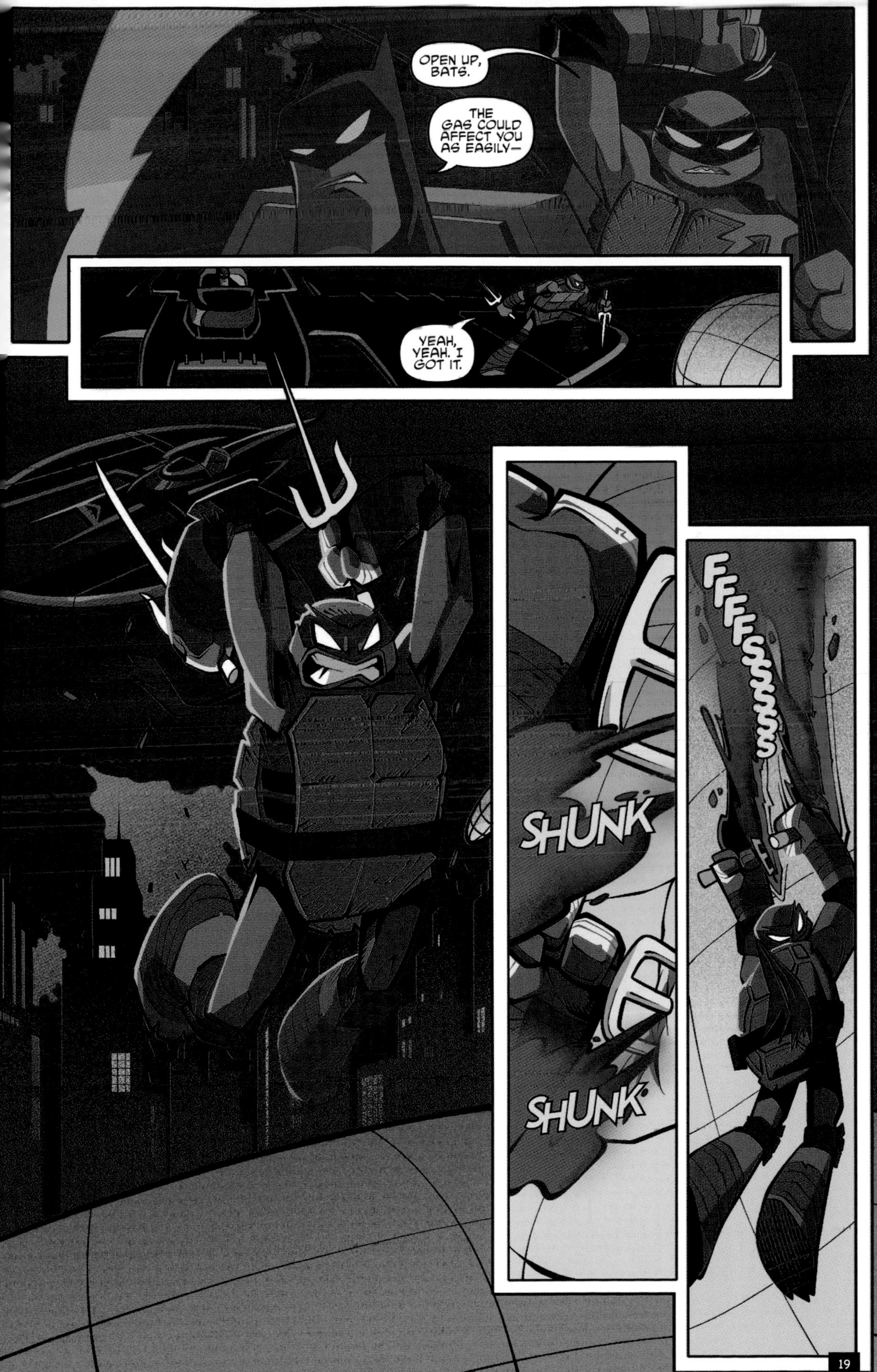
OPEN UP, BATS.
THE GAS COULD AFFECT YOU AS EASILY—
YEAH, YEAH. I GOT IT.
SHUNK
SHUNK
FFFFSSSSSS

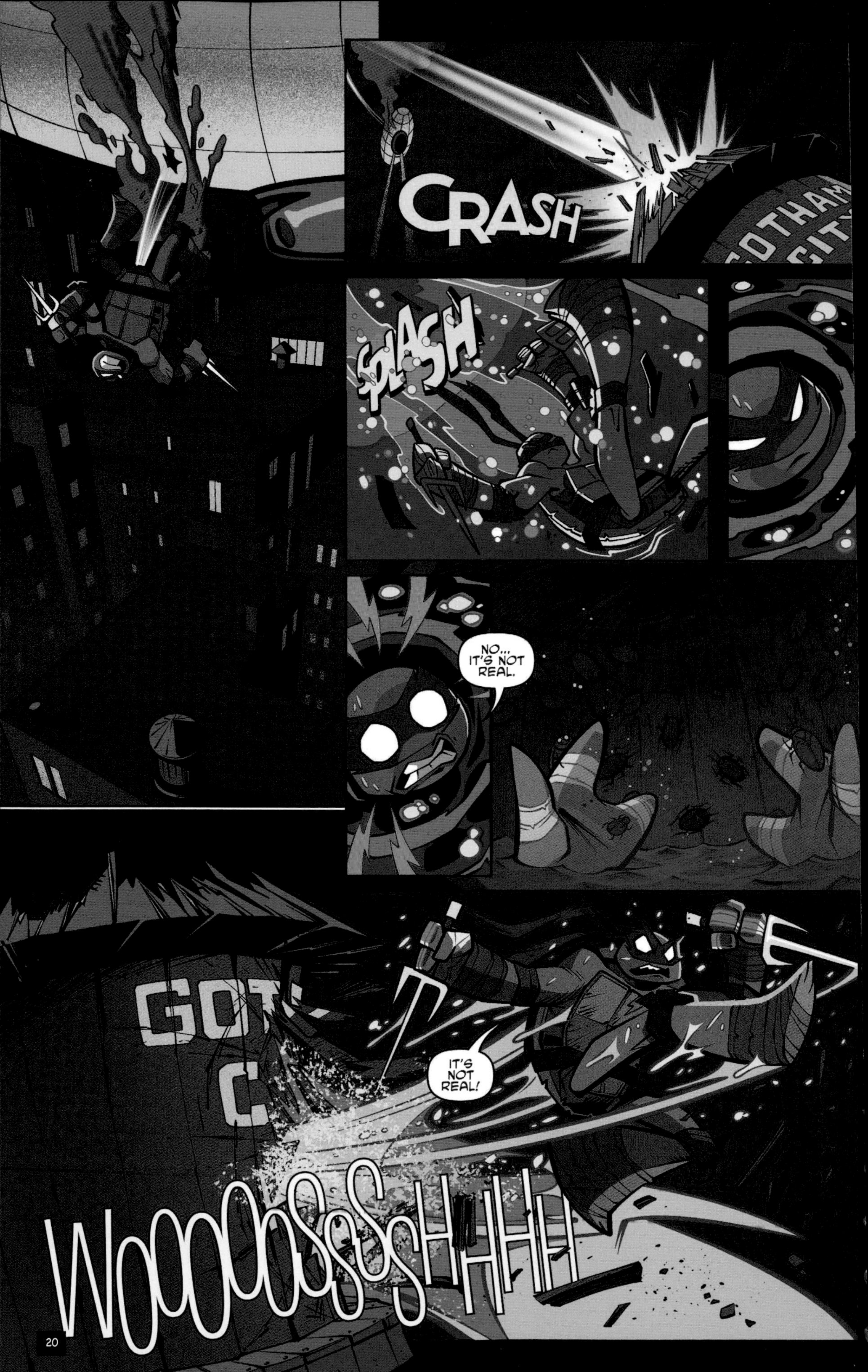
CRASH
GOTHAM CITY
SPLASH
NO... IT'S NOT REAL.
GOT
C
IT'S NOT REAL!
WOOOOOSSSSHHHHH

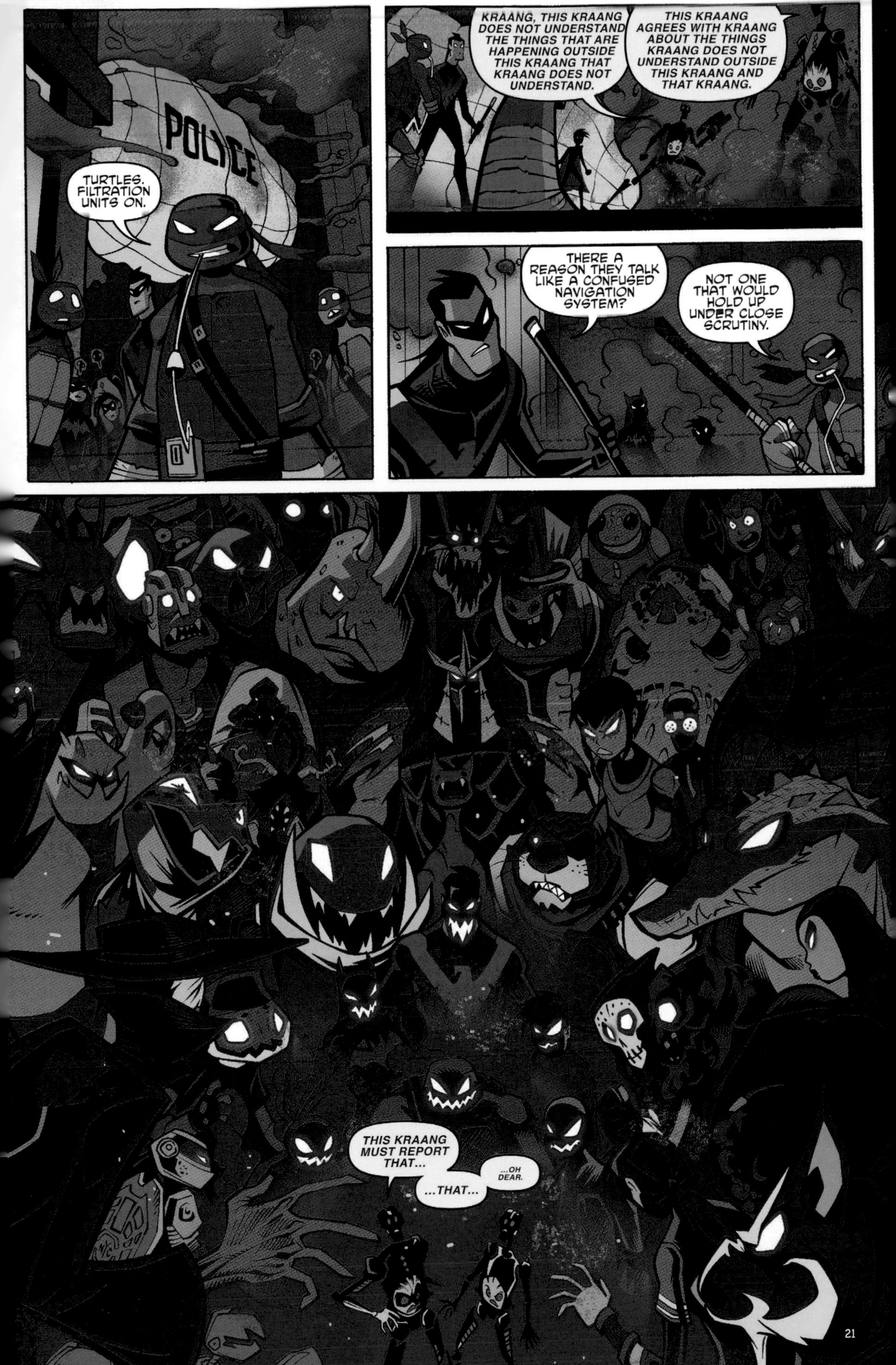
TURTLES. FILTRATION UNITS ON.
KRAANG, THIS KRAANG DOES NOT UNDERSTAND THE THINGS THAT ARE HAPPENING OUTSIDE THIS KRAANG THAT KRAANG DOES NOT UNDERSTAND.
THIS KRAANG AGREES WITH KRAANG ABOUT THE THINGS KRAANG DOES NOT UNDERSTAND OUTSIDE THIS KRAANG AND THAT KRAANG.
THERE A REASON THEY TALK LIKE A CONFUSED NAVIGATION SYSTEM?
NOT ONE THAT WOULD HOLD UP UNDER CLOSE SCRUTINY.
POLICE
THIS KRAANG MUST REPORT THAT...
...THAT...
...OH DEAR.

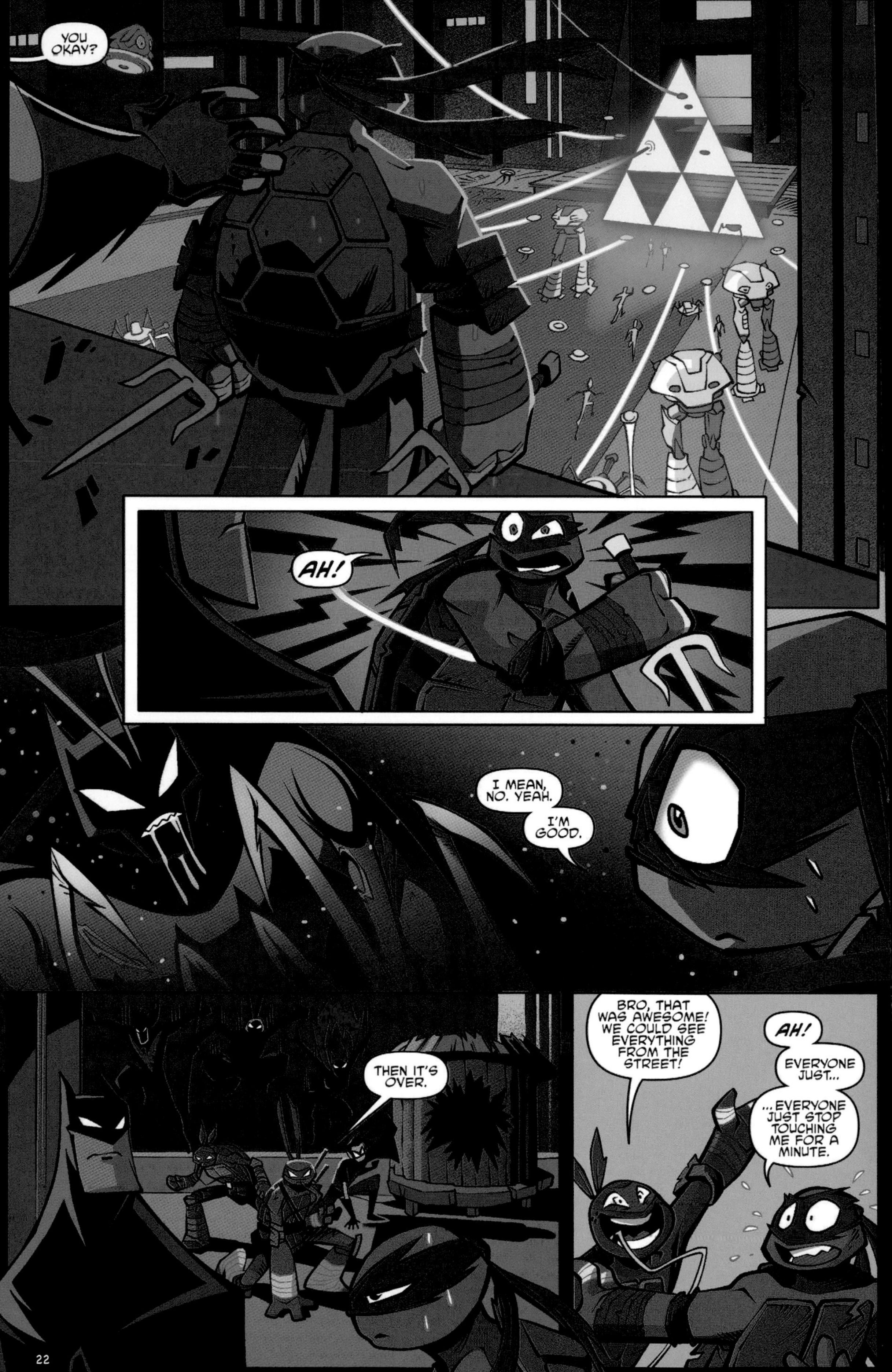

YOU OKAY?
AH!
I MEAN, NO. YEAH.
I'M GOOD.
THEN IT'S OVER.
BRO, THAT WAS AWESOME! WE COULD SEE EVERYTHING FROM THE STREET!
AH!
EVERYONE JUST...
...EVERYONE JUST STOP TOUCHING ME FOR A MINUTE.

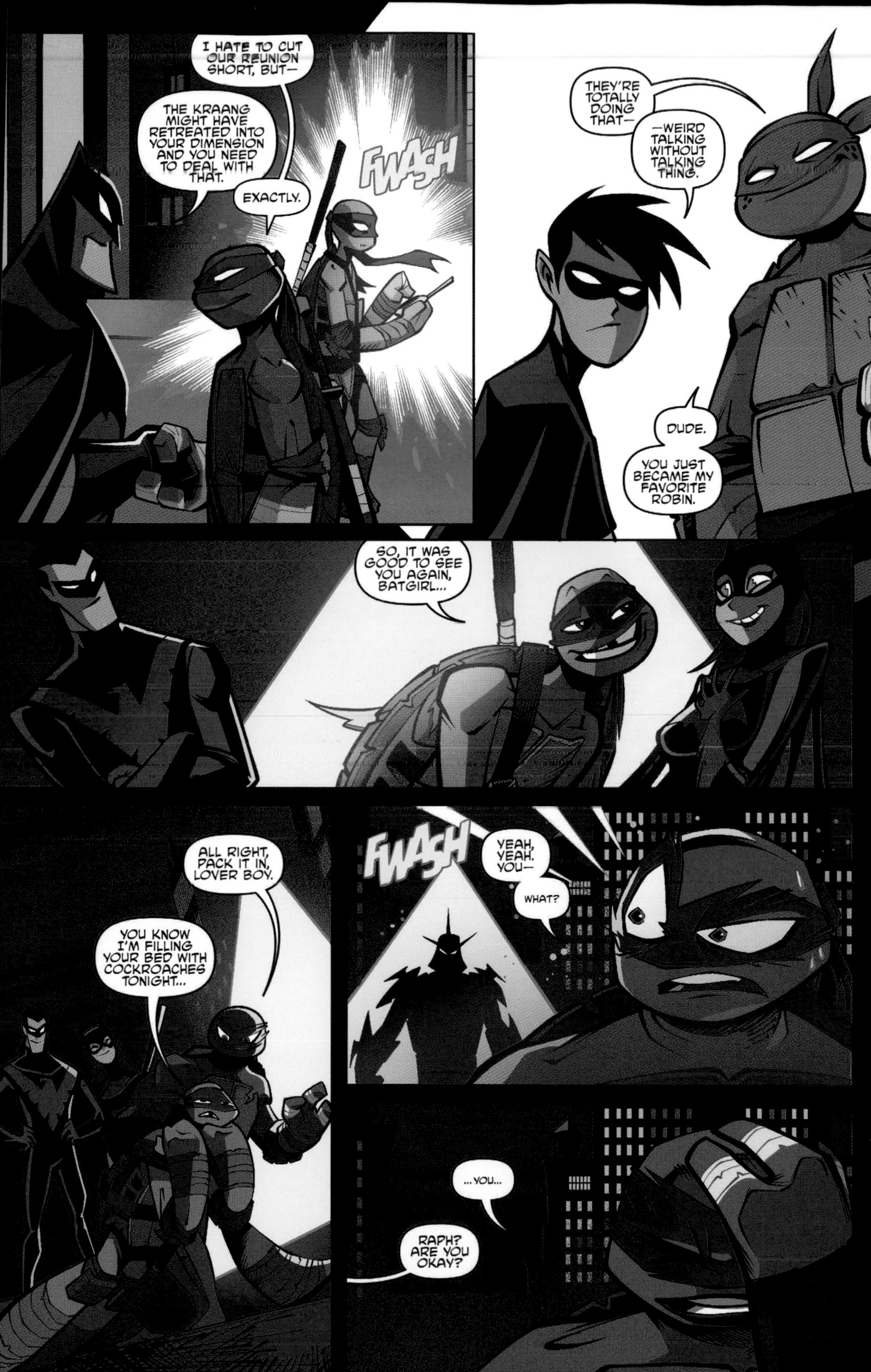
I HATE TO CUT OUR REUNION SHORT, BUT—
THE KRAANG MIGHT HAVE RETREATED INTO YOUR DIMENSION AND YOU NEED TO DEAL WITH THAT.
EXACTLY.
FWASH
THEY'RE TOTALLY DOING THAT—
—WEIRD TALKING WITHOUT TALKING THING.
DUDE.
YOU JUST BECAME MY FAVORITE ROBIN.
SO, IT WAS GOOD TO SEE YOU AGAIN, BATGIRL...
ALL RIGHT, PACK IT IN, LOVER BOY.
YOU KNOW I'M FILLING YOUR BED WITH COCKROACHES TONIGHT...
FWASH
YEAH, YEAH. YOU—
WHAT?
...YOU...
RAPH? ARE YOU OKAY?

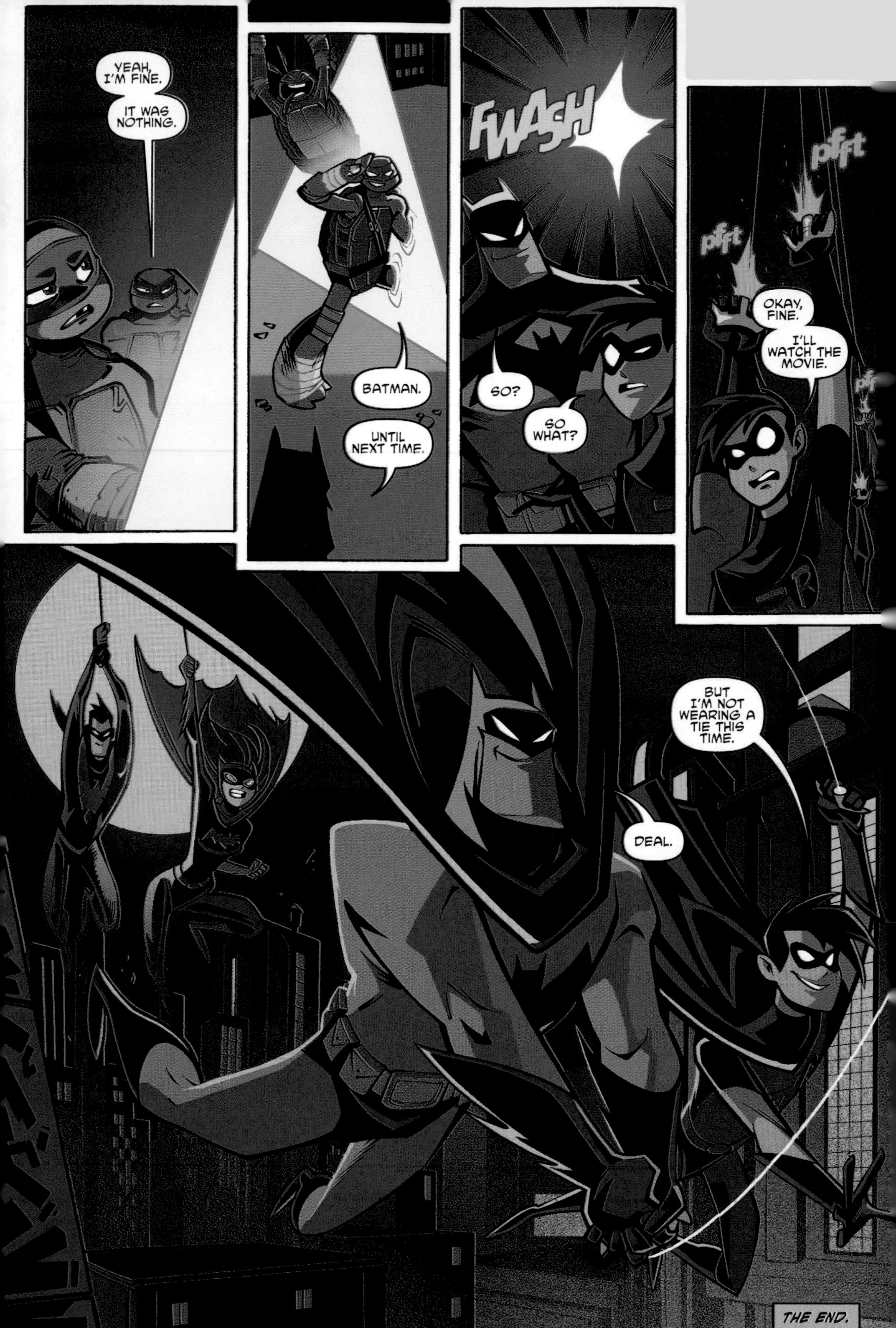
YEAH, I'M FINE.
IT WAS NOTHING.
BATMAN.
UNTIL NEXT TIME.
FWASH
SO?
SO WHAT?
pfft
pfft
OKAY, FINE.
I'LL WATCH THE MOVIE.
BUT I'M NOT WEARING A TIE THIS TIME.
DEAL.
THE END.

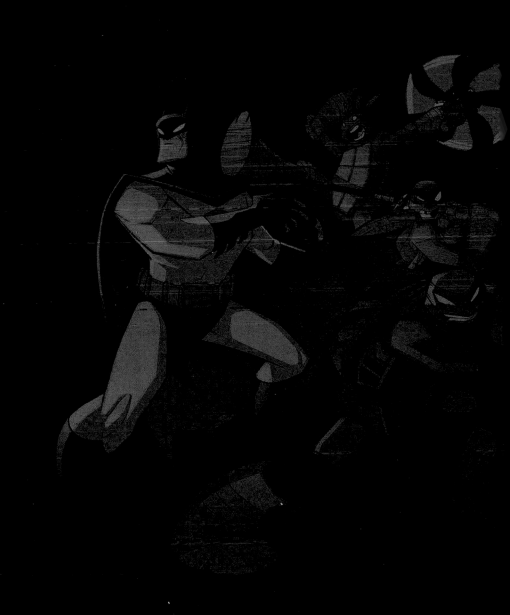

CREATOR

MATTHEW K. MANNING

THE AUTHOR OF THE AMAZON BEST-SELLING HARDCOVER *BATMAN: A VISUAL HISTORY*,
MATTHEW K. MANNING HAS CONTRIBUTED TO MANY COMIC BOOKS, INCLUDING *BEWARE
THE BATMAN*, *SPIDER-MAN UNLIMITED*, *PIRATES OF THE CARIBBEAN: SIX SEA SHANTIES*,
JUSTICE LEAGUE ADVENTURES, *LOONEY TUNES*, AND *SCOOBY-DOO, WHERE ARE YOU?*
WHEN NOT WRITING COMICS, MANNING OFTEN AUTHORS BOOKS ABOUT COMICS, AS WELL
AS A SERIES OF YOUNG READER BOOKS STARRING SUPERMAN, BATMAN, AND THE FLASH
FOR CAPSTONE. HE CURRENTLY RESIDES IN ASHEVILLE, NORTH CAROLINA, WITH HIS WIFE,
DOROTHY, AND THEIR TWO DAUGHTERS, LILLIAN AND GWENDOLYN. VISIT HIM ONLINE AT
WWW.MATTHEWKMANNING.COM.

JON SOMMARIVA

JON SOMMARIVA WAS BORN IN SYDNEY, AUSTRALIA. HE HAS BEEN DRAWING COMIC
BOOKS SINCE 2002. HIS WORK CAN BE SEEN IN *GEMINI*, *REXODUS*, *TMNT ADVENTURES*,
AND *STAR WARS ADVENTURES*, AMONG OTHER COMICS. WHEN HE IS NOT DRAWING, HE
ENJOYS WATCHING MOVIES AND PLAYING WITH HIS SON, FELIX.

GLOSSARY

android (AN-droid)—a robot that looks, thinks, and acts very similar to a human being

brilliant (BRIL-yuhnt)—shining very brightly

concoction (kon-KOK-shuhn)—a mixture using many ingredients

defunct (di-FUNKT)—no longer useful or usable

dirigible (DEER-uh-juh-buhl)—an aircraft that is lighter than air and that can be steered

en route (AHN ROOT)—on the way

fidgety (FIJ-it-ee)—in a state where you keep moving out of boredom

filtration (fil-TRAY-shun)—the act or process of cleaning air

horde (HORD)—a group so large it cannot be counted

malfunctioning (mal-FUHNGK-shun-ing)—failing to work correctly

notorious (noh-TOH-ree-uhs)—being well known for something bad

preposterous (pree-POSS-tur-uhss)—ridiculous and absurd

renegade (REN-uh-gayd)—a rebel

vent (VENT)—an opening where steam, smoke, or gas is released

VISUAL QUESTIONS AND WRITING PROMPTS

1. WHY DO YOU THINK BATMAN IS AMUSED AT WHAT ROBIN IS SAYING HERE?

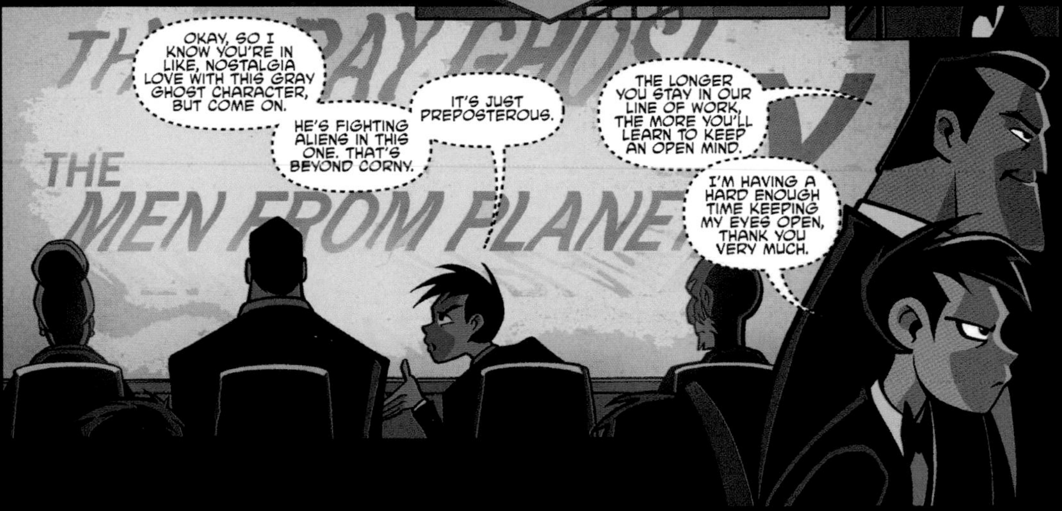
THE GRAY GHOST
THE MEN FROM PLANET
OKAY, SO I KNOW YOU'RE IN LIKE, NOSTALGIA LOVE WITH THIS GRAY GHOST CHARACTER, BUT COME ON.
HE'S FIGHTING ALIENS IN THIS ONE. THAT'S BEYOND CORNY.
IT'S JUST PREPOSTEROUS.
THE LONGER YOU STAY IN OUR LINE OF WORK, THE MORE YOU'LL LEARN TO KEEP AN OPEN MIND.
I'M HAVING A HARD ENOUGH TIME KEEPING MY EYES OPEN, THANK YOU VERY MUCH.

2. WHICH SILHOUETTE BELONGS TO WHICH CHARACTERS? HOW DO YOU KNOW?

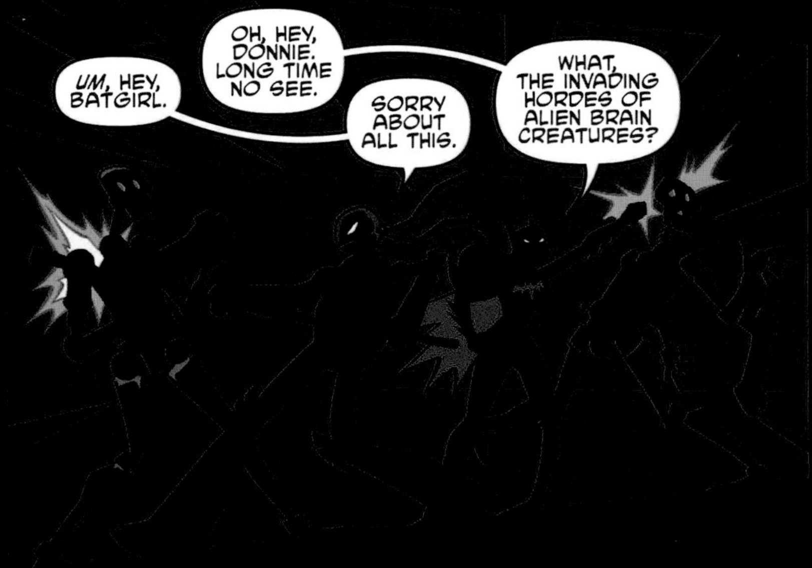
UM, HEY, BATGIRL.
OH, HEY, DONNIE. LONG TIME NO SEE.
SORRY ABOUT ALL THIS.
WHAT, THE INVADING HORDES OF ALIEN BRAIN CREATURES?

3. WHAT WAS THE JOKER THINKING WHILE LISTENING TO SCARECROW'S CONVERSATION WITH BATMAN AND RAPHAEL?

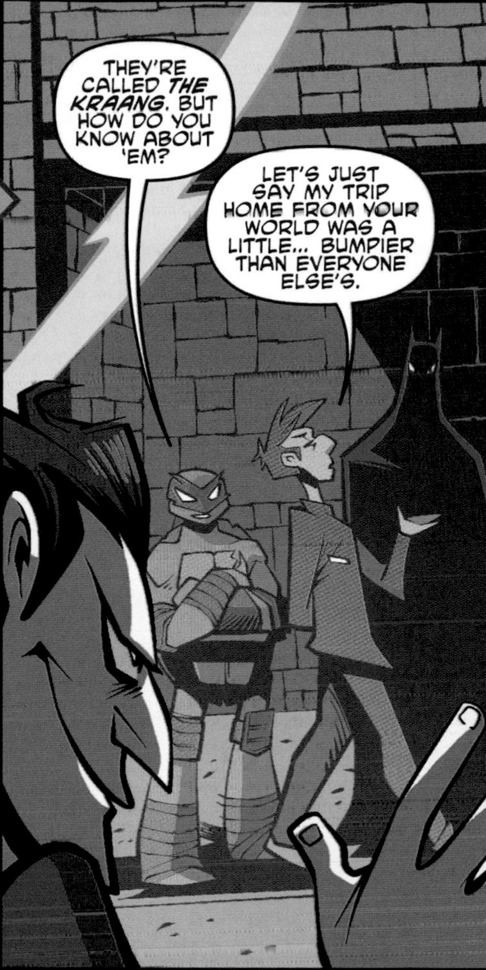

THEY'RE CALLED *THE KRAANG*. BUT HOW DO YOU KNOW ABOUT 'EM?
LET'S JUST SAY MY TRIP HOME FROM YOUR WORLD WAS A LITTLE... BUMPIER THAN EVERYONE ELSE'S.

4. BASED ON EACH CHARACTER'S FACIAL EXPRESSION AND BODY LANGUAGE BELOW, WHAT DO YOU THINK NIGHTWING, DONATELLO, AND BATGIRL ARE THINKING?

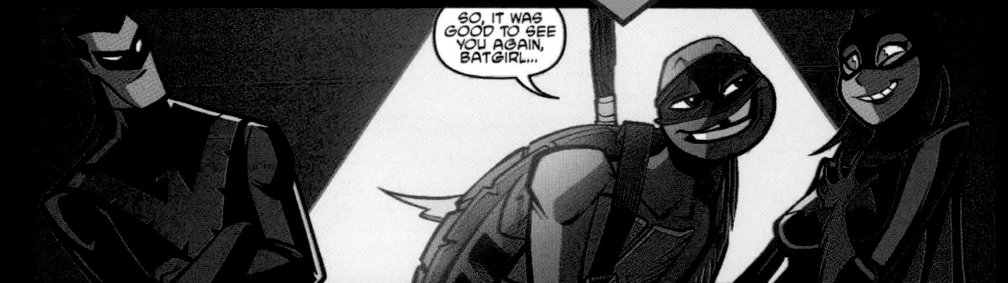

SO, IT WAS GOOD TO SEE YOU AGAIN, BATGIRL...

BATMAN TEENAGE MUTANT NINJA TURTLES ADVENTURES

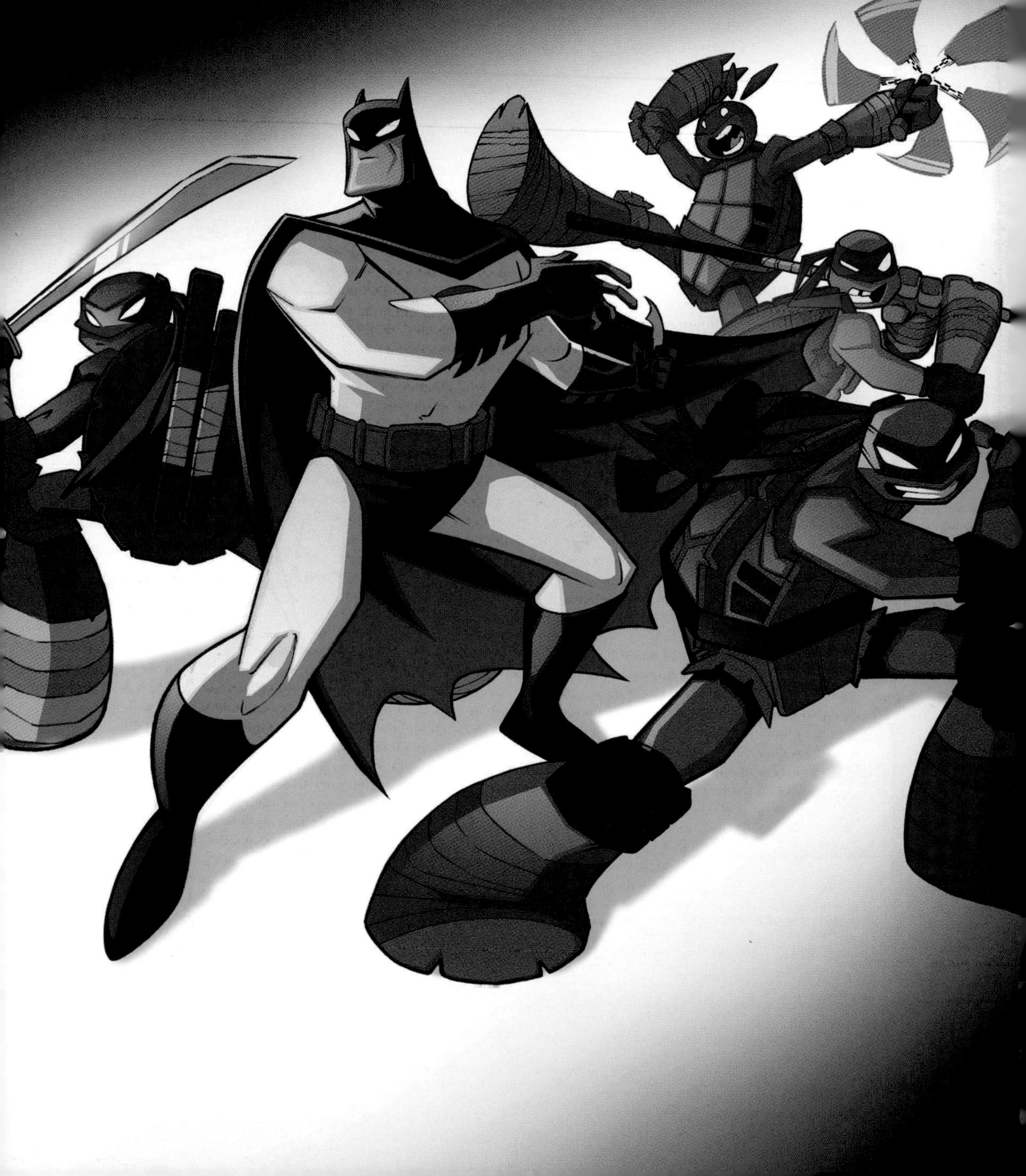

READ THEM ALL!

IDW
BATMAN TEENAGE MUTANT NINJA TURTLES ADVENTURES
THE FACE OF TWO WORLDS

IDW
BATMAN TEENAGE MUTANT NINJA TURTLES ADVENTURES
THE CLOWN AND THE CLAN

IDW
BATMAN TEENAGE MUTANT NINJA TURTLES ADVENTURES
GREENER ON THE OTHER SIDE

IDW
BATMAN TEENAGE MUTANT NINJA TURTLES ADVENTURES
TO LAUGH SO NOT TO CRY

IDW
BATMAN TEENAGE MUTANT NINJA TURTLES ADVENTURES
THROUGH THE LOOKING GLASS

IDW
BATMAN TEENAGE MUTANT NINJA TURTLES ADVENTURES
THE TERROR OF THE KRAANG

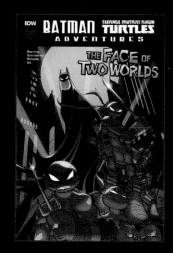

BATMAN. TEENAGE MUTANT NINJA TURTLES

ADVENTURES